Contents

A Fault to Fear

BOOK 3 OF THE SPIRIT WIND SERIES

DANIEL DYDEK

BEORN PUBLISHING, LLC

Chapter 9

The weather continued to turn, growing bitterly cold. Snows flurried but did not stick as slate gray skies hid sun and moon. Mahmoud glanced skyward often, grumbling to himself, and often in Arabic. Our donkey plodded steadily though, tail clamped against gusts of wind that swirled my skirts at times and chilled my legs.

Always when I asked, Castle Fosse was "just ahead." It was rare that I appreciated Mahmoud's attempts to make the journey seem easier. By the fifth night, I stopped asking.

For Thomas and I...it felt often like nothing had changed. Proper inns were few and far between. More often than not we partook of a stranger's kindness, sleeping in haymows or spare beds. While we could—and did—share the bed, sometimes Mahmoud was there too on the other side of Thomas, or within arm's reach.

And...Thomas had not healed overnight either. Even in the one inn we found our third day south from Aurden he slept beside me as a brother in a too-crowded house. I knew perhaps we might. And I was grateful mostly to be able to tell the odd concerned farmwife that no, we were wed, and it was perfectly acceptable to share their hastily-made pallet.

He had taken to walking in front of me—to protect me, I suppose. I was not ungrateful, for the wind howled most days. But with no touch, no glances, very few words, it felt as his wife just as it had as his friend. And some days it was worse.

And so, one morning, as I followed dutifully along, I slowed as they slowed. Distracted by my thoughts, I didn't look around until the land bent sharply upward. Then as I toiled, feet trying to slip on a thin coat of snow, I finally looked to see how far we had to climb. It was a tall ridge, cloaked in trees. The road went up for a time, then turned finally and back across the face.

"Are we entering mountains?" I asked.

Mahmoud glanced back, his dark eyes glittering as he searched mine. "No," he said finally, turning forward again. "Not yet."

I glanced at Thomas, who gave a brief grin that stabbed my heart. I saw him again at the door of the convent, kind eyes and warm smile flashing, my heart pattering. Certainly not the future I had envisioned, and all because Judith! And not just her, of course: the Sisters too, allowing it. Thomas, allowing at least some. Was he even trying to heal? To be a husband to me in more than just word?

I felt my lips tremble and looked away. His kiss on our wedding day had shot me skyward. But, like the arrow, I quickly fell and furrowed into the dirt again. We had not kissed since.

I glanced furtively to see if he noticed the emotions I knew were playing across my face, but his eyes were ahead again. There was an eager spring to his step. I grit my teeth.

The road climbed interminably, and I began to pant. But we all plodded onward as the wind picked up. The sun was behind a far mountain and long shadows stretched over the land. I could look down, now, to the plain we had just crossed, the road lifting gently back the way we had come.

I sighed shortly, between gasps, and felt for the flame inside. It rose gently to meet me.

Wherefore lift up the hands which hang down, and the feeble knees, lest any root of bitterness springing up trouble you, and thereby many be defiled.

Feeble knees, I definitely had. I liked that part. The bitterness? Well, at the convent I would have said I earned it. But that the Sacred Fire spoke it to me now meant I had not. I closed my eyes, bent my will to the Word. *I cannot cut out this root alone, not when it sprouts so easily.*

The flame burned brighter. With closed eyes I could almost see it. I certainly apprehended it, full of oranges and blues. Within the rush I thought I sensed music, too. I hummed to myself one of the hymns we had learned at the convent. Quietly at first, but as the fire mounted I hummed louder still, to hear my own voice.

Another voice met mine, and I looked up as Thomas hummed the hymn along with me. His eyes were still ahead, watching the road, and yet he joined in. And, I saw, we were suddenly near the top of the ridge.

I longed to reach out and grasp Thomas' hand, pouring myself into the hymn as I felt the root spring up again. Mahmoud glanced back, and I worried he would be annoyed. But he merely watched us, then turned us around the last curve as the road crested the ridge.

We paused as the trees opened up, looking down at Castle Fosse.

It lay in the center of a broad valley, narrow at the head but widening quickly. A stream which began in the mountains—I could see them now far to our left—flowed down the center, split around the black stones and spires of the castle, then rejoined and flowed out of sight where the valley bent south. Broad, fertile fields—blank and snow-covered now—lay around the castle, no less than twenty farmhouses that I could see dotting the landscape.

The wind abruptly fell away, all sound silenced. I barely noticed at first, until the silence thickened like a blanket, grew heavier. I moved toward Thomas, did not even hear my feet on the stones. Our donkey shook himself, but no tack jingled—his breath gusting into the cold did not snort.

I moved into Thomas' sight, and he turned to look at me. I saw in his eyes the recognition that the silence affected him, too. Mahmoud's lips parted, and though he spoke his mouth worked slowly.

Faintly, above the silence, or perhaps behind it, there came almost a terrible shriek. Yet it was not muffled, or faint by distance, and it did not echo as it should in a valley like this. Thomas and I both looked toward the castle again.

Suddenly, against one of its towers, I saw a shape writhe. A long, sinuous body wrapped around the tower, scales rippling in fir green and black mottle. Peering over the top was a massive head like I had never seen except in the illumination of some of the manuscripts left over from the monastery. It seemed the shriek emanated from the beast, though it still resonated only in the background. Now it felt, as I stared at it, as though the muffling silence was indeed pushed forth by this terrible creature. It scanned the valley floor, then the hills. I shrank against Thomas as its piercing gaze swept closer and closer toward us. The shriek briefly crescendoed, then passed away again. My breath froze in my throat, fearing what might happen if he looked directly at us.

But before he did, the shriek fell away and normal sounds returned. I sucked in a deep breath as the winged serpent climbed into the tower and disappeared.

Mahmoud was staring at us, waiting for an answer. I looked up at Thomas, who looked down at me, his eyes searching mine. He flashed a brief, regretful smile at me as his hand slid across my cheek. I managed to lean into it quickly before it was gone.

"Sorry, Mahmoud," he said, all normal smiles now. "I haven't seen a castle like it! What did you say?"

"Night, it falls fast while we stand here, and the cold," he said. As he pushed past, leading the donkey, he cast me a swift glance of warning. "I hope nothing is wrong?" he asked as he continued down the road.

"Nothing yet," I said. Thomas passed in front of me too, and when I looked down again even the tower the dragon rested on was gone as though it had never existed. *Good thing the weapons we fight with are not against flesh and blood,* I thought. Thomas' sword would be useless if we actually needed to fight such a creature. *But what is it doing here?*

As we descended, the valley fell deeper into shadow. Farther and farther away the river glittered where the sun still reached it. And, it struck me particularly, some of the ramparts gleamed like the teeth of a maw at heights where the sun still shone.

When we reached the bottom of the ridge and set out along the road that ran straight toward the moat, Thomas fell back until he was nearly beside me. "You did see the same thing as I did, right?" he asked.

I nodded. "If you saw a tower that is no longer there," I added, since he wasn't looking at me and because I didn't know if he had actually seen it or not either.

His pace faltered and suddenly I was beside him. "A tower?" he asked, resuming his steps. "Not...I mean, is that what you saw?"

"Well, what did you see?"

His eyes cast between me and Mahmoud. "I'm... Maybe I'm not sure."

I held my breath a moment. "Thomas," I said, failing to keep a tone out of my voice. To his credit he recognized it, and looked at me earnestly. "This is me," I continued, more gently. Then, just a little harder: "Your wife."

His fingers flexed on his sword. "I'm sorry," he said. "I guess—I thought I saw a small child on the ramparts of the keep." His eyes flickered toward it. When I looked, I saw nothing at first—but my tower was still gone, too. But when I glanced again at him he stiffened. Looking ahead I saw it: a small child, a girl I thought, her summer dress blowing in a breeze we couldn't feel. A dress far too light for this weather. A muffled cry drifted down to us, did not seem to strike Mahmoud, and when it faded away so did the girl.

"Oh," I said.

His eyes, now wide, were where my tower was, and his Adam's apple bobbed. "Oh," he said, a bit more breathlessly than mine had been.

"Yes," I replied.

"Okay, then. This should be interesting."

I could only cock an eyebrow.

Soon we were passing through the gate. A pair of guards hailed us and we stopped. "Mahmoud," one said, a squat man nearly wide as he was tall. His eyes ran over the mule's packs, to Mahmoud, and flicked quickly to us. "Part of your wares?"

"No, captain. They wanted it, to come with me. Some business to the south."

He looked us over more thoroughly, his eyes lingering on Thomas' sword. "Well?" he asked gruffly. "What answer do you have for yourselves?"

But speak...

"We've come to see your lord about his tower," I said quickly as Thomas' mouth opened. All eyes turned to me, but I held the captain's gaze. "The east tower."

His face paled a moment—frightening to see on one of his obvious experience. "Then come with me," he said. He turned, bellowed as we passed under the gate for a replacement, and began to lead us up the road to the keep.

Behind, the portcullis slammed closed. I startled, looked around. Everyone acted as though that were normal. I understood it was growing dark, especially in the valley, but the sky was bright overhead, and Scuros had definitely not rung. I could see the chapel's bell tower, silent and stark as it sat in silhouette. The streets were emptying in an almost furtive haste. Distracted as I was, I didn't notice at first that our captain had quickened his steps as well—not until my breath came in gasps. We pressed on.

Finally the keep rose before us. The captain looked east, muttering. I followed his gaze, saw the remnants of some scaffolding near a wall, it appeared. But only the edges remained. A man was standing near it, long dark hair thin against his shoulders. He peered at us, then scurried off.

"Who was that?" I asked.

"Amaury. That scaffolding...we thought we would need additional ramparts on the wall. A spot our archers could shoot from. So his Lordship had it built."

"Was it deemed unnecessary?"

The captain's face darkened. "The scaffolding fell," he said. "Poorly constructed. It nearly killed... Well, we did not try again."

"And what's Amaury doing these days?" Thomas muttered.

The captain glanced back, his mouth twisted. He quickly straightened it. "Not my place," he said.

Thomas' eyebrows climbed. "He's still a master mason?"

"Journeyman," he corrected quickly, then clamped his lips shut.

Our Father maketh his sun to rise on the evil and on the good," I offered.

"Or someone does," the captain muttered.

Then we were bustling inside the doors, and those too were booming shut as great timbers were thrown across them. We were in an open forecourt, the keep proper still ahead of us. But the captain turned, giving us an apologetic smile. "Gets dreadfully dark out there, here between the high places. May we take your mule, please?"

All of the hurry was gone from his demeanor, and even those moving here and there through the forecourt seemed at their leisure. Mahmoud handed over the reins without question. As our mule clopped across the stones, Thomas and I glanced at each other, and he shrugged. *If Mahmoud seems at ease...but then, he gave nothing away in Aurden.* My hand went unconsciously to my face. Much harm had come from trusting Mahmoud's instincts already on this journey.

Thomas' gaze softened toward me, and I dropped my hand. I turned my gaze to the captain. "There can be much other fear in the dark," I said. "But to those in The Beloved comes much comfort and safe-keeping."

His smile, though persistent, seemed strained. "Of course," he said. "But let us be inside, out of the cold. Dinner, I believe, is soon served. And you'll need to meet his Lord and Lady Pendrel."

We went, and as the inner doors closed behind us it felt—by contrast—nearly like entering a furnace. Tapestries bedecked the walls against drafts, and even in this antechamber I could hear the fires from the dining hall roaring.

The captain led us all forward, but near the double-leaved doors turned us right and down a hallway. "You'll want to refresh yourselves from the road, first," he said. "My lordship maintains a good keep: you should find clothes aplenty, and warm water for washing. Will you be needing two or three rooms?" he asked, looking at Thomas.

I suppose he only hesitated a moment—just long enough to indicate we were only newly-wed. But to my shame it felt like he had clear forgotten. "Two, yes," he said finally, glancing quickly at me with a smile. "Rae-Anna is my wife."

"Of course. For you, here then," he said, gesturing to a door. A liveried servant materialized from some nook and opened the door ahead of us. As we went inside, Mahmoud was led down the hall by another servant.

For the next few moments the servant bustled silently around the room, lighting the rushes and stoking a fire in the small hearth. Every now and again I caught her surreptitious glance toward an arrow-slit gradually growing darker. She swung a kettle to the fire, to let the water inside warm. Finally she opened a small trunk, displaying folded clothing inside. She pulled out several towels of thick cotton, setting them on a small stand near the fire to warm as well. She briefly met our eyes—I thought I saw a worry in them, veiled but out of place—curtsied, and departed. As the door swung closed I saw the captain still outside, waiting with arms folded.

I sat on a stool and wrenched at my boots. As I began on my stockings, Thomas smiled but turned away. "Did you notice the servant?" he asked. "I understand a fear of darkness, but here..."

"Thomas," I said quietly. Hurt. "You're allowed to look, you know."

His shoulders hunched as his head turned only halfway toward me. I still could not see his eyes. "I know."

I waited a few moments longer, then resumed with blurred vision.

I washed quickly with the water, barely tepid as yet, dried even faster, and donned the provided garments. They fit well enough, though I was sure to stand out amongst the other castle guests as the hose bunched here and there, and the bodice sagged in places not fashionable. The laces were drawn as tight as they could go. But it would serve.

Still silent, I strode past Thomas and stood for his turn, facing resolutely away. Every rustle of his clothing and splash of water hit my ears like a shout, slicing my heart for what he still denied us. Once I was tempted to turn and try to catch him, just to prove it would be okay. But whether through bitterness or prudence I did not.

I cleared my throat. "Do you think the dragon prowls the night?" I asked. "Perhaps everyone must be indoors before dark for that reason."

"It could be," he said. I briefly hated him for how normal his voice sounded. "And why the girl on the ramparts?"

I shook my head. "Twice so far my mission has begun in confusion. I'm almost not surprised—"

"Our mission?" Thomas asked.

I blinked, turned my head halfway just as he had, without looking toward him. "This time, I suppose," I said carelessly.

"Hmm."

His hand on my arm startled me and I turned, my gaze going instantly into his hazel eyes. I was prepared for defiance, felt my own back begin to stiffen. But then he leaned in and kissed me, still gently, as he gathered me in his arms. When he finally pulled away my heart was giddy.

"Remember that my part in your story began with you telling me about some strange blue fire lighting your hand," he said quietly. "And in Aurden I was spelled by a centuries-old demon. I am sorry

I was absent from your beginnings, but mine were still very confusing."

My vision blurred again, for very different reasons this time, as my head hung. His strong, farmer-turned-warrior hand cupped my chin and brought my face back up and he kissed me again, briefly. He wiped my tears until I could see his smile again. "As for the other thing...well, now is not exactly the right time anyway. But I promise I have not forgotten, nor do I stop seeking The Beloved for the healing we both wish for."

"I'm sorry, Thomas," I managed. "I just wish Judith and the others—"

"I know." His voice hardened, though his hand was still gentle on my cheek.

A knock at the door interrupted us, and the captain's voice came from outside. "Pardon you both," he called, "but though dinner will not wait on you, it would be unseemly to arrive late. And there is still the...matter, to bring before his lordship."

I stepped away from Thomas with a deep breath, wiped at my own face this time. I nodded at him with a smile, and he went to the door.

It was time to see what the lord of the manor knew about his invisible tower.

Chapter 2

We all three trailed behind the captain as he brought us back to the main doors. He whispered aside to the door-keeper—presumably some sort of steward—then waited with hands clasped demurely before him as the keeper ducked inside.

As we waited, suddenly he turned back to us. "Mahmoud is known to us," he said, glancing quickly at him. "So by his presence you are vouched for. That and your...special knowledge." This time his piercing gaze found me. "But in our strange times, forgive me if I stay nearby. Armed."

"Of course, Captain...?"

He looked me up and down. "Boris."

I smiled as he turned away to face the doors. Soon the keeper came out and nodded. Captain Boris preceded us, though as soon as we were inside Mahmoud went and sat at the lower end of the two long tables before us. Boris led us along the right-hand side, to approach the table set crosswise on the dais, where I presumed sat Lord and Lady Pendrel. There were some others near them, though two empty chairs sat directly to Lord Pendrel's left hand.

The fires were indeed roaring, the heat hitting me nearly like a large hand. Countless candles and rushes brightly lit the rest of the hall, and I could see no dark shadows anywhere—excepting, perhaps, in a few of the haunted eyes of those gathered along the tables. Besides the two long rows there were scattered other tables, in every hollow and fold of the hall, packed round about with even more people. Even if the entire village had gathered in this hall—and I assumed they had—there bespoke even more. And I wondered if we were not the only travelers who had stopped in out of the cold.

As we mounted the stairs to the dais, Lord Pendrel stood and smiled. "Be welcome to our hall," he said in a voice to carry throughout the room—surely for the benefit of everyone gathered, not us alone. "Myself and the Lady Pendrel foresaw such days, and you will not find us lacking." His voice lowered to normal tones as we bowed, led still by Boris. "And I am told you come to us bearing—if not tidings, some knowledge which we did not know anyone else possessed."

"What I have comes by The Beloved," I said. His Lordship's eyes left Thomas and fastened to me. To his credit, looking full on my scarred face did not seem to unnerve him. "And through his Sacred Fire. Though," I continued, smiling, "oft times the knowledge is incomplete, and he permits others to fill in gaps where they might."

Lord Pendrel gestured to the seats beside him before finding his own again. After we sat, Boris close by but standing to the rear, Lord Pendrel glanced to her Ladyship, received a gracious nod in return, and rang a bell. Side doors far down the hall snapped open and the dinner began.

When he had said we would not find his hall lacking, he had not exaggerated. Platter after platter proceeded out of those doors, borne by a seemingly endless stream of servants. A separate, select group tended the raised table where we sat. Our goblets held wine where the others held ale or water; our meats came prepared a little more delicately, or intricately, while theirs was only sliced. Steaming, to be sure, and dripping in every bit as much gravy. But sliced. Fruits, nuts, and vegetables covered whatever parts of the table were left after the meats were set down. And, as soon as his Lordship put the first skewer to his mouth, the rest of those gathered began their own tasks with no more call for decorum.

I couldn't help but observe her Ladyship as I ate—reveled in foods I had never before tasted. I hesitated over the wine, forcefully banishing my memory from Aurden before sipping. This one was not as dry as Paulo's had been, though it was just as clear, and tasted more of grape than apple. But it suited the rest of the meal, I felt—and didn't immediately attack my senses. Her Ladyship sipped infrequently, only picked now and again at her food. Rarely, in my glances, did I see her eat, though her plate gradually diminished. And despite her smiles and comments to some of her ladies-in-waiting, there was a sadness there that broke through from time to time.

Finally, as some plates emptied and servants took them away, Lord Pendrel turned to me and Thomas. "Captain Boris tells me you come lately from—where was it? Holden? And through Aurden?"

I touched a napkin to my mouth. "Yes, Lordship. I was in service to be a Sister at the convent outside Holden. But The Beloved's call on me was...distinct, from theirs."

He looked to Thomas. "So your wedding, then, is more recent."

"Yes, Lordship," Thomas answered, giving me a soft smile. "Just before we left Aurden."

"How is it, then, you know of the tower?"

Some clattering ceased, and I glanced across to see her Ladyship staring intently, still through her smile.

"We observed it, your Lordship, as we came over the ridge."

"Only the tower?" he asked, innocuously enough. A few more skewers went silent, so he picked up another and took a bite. The eating around him resumed.

I also took the opportunity to take a small bite, to help in the appearance we only exchanged pleasantries. After a quick swallow, I said, "No, Lordship."

"Fascinating," he said, glancing around the room. "Would you be surprised to hear you are one of the few? To see it, at least. All have felt his presence. But I had thought the sight of him was a special burden for her Ladyship and myself alone." He shook his head, took a bite of bread and chewed thoughtfully.

"Lordship," Thomas cut in quietly. "The tower and its inhabitant is not all we saw."

The smiles disappeared from both Pendrels. His Lordship swallowed hard, and when he spoke I could tell he fought his voice. "Was it not?"

"Have any others seen her, as well?" I asked.

Lord Pendrel looked away. The feast in the hall raised in volume earnestly, then. Lady Pendrel looked hard at us. "That is our curse, alone," she said.

His Lordship's fist tightened on his goblet, and he raised it shakily to his lips as he drank. "This wine," he whispered, "is most excellent. I knew it would keep well." He cleared his throat, strengthened his voice. "I was a vintner, in my youth. Dabbled, at first; many are the duties of a young lordling." He smiled at us. "But my father was a consummate manor-lord. There was little for me to do, while he ruled—outside of learning from him. And so I took up a study of wines. This is not my own—of course my duties increased since his death—and yet I knew when I tested the casks..."

"I have little experience," I said. "But I feel I see what you mean." A platter rang as it struck the floor; a flustered servant scooped it up and ducked through the door. While his Lord and Ladyship glanced over, they made no special comment.

"Did your Lord and Ladyship forget to lighten that platter?" a new voice rang out. I glanced toward the doors, saw Thome Fool enter in his motley. "Shame, that; mustn't leave that which should be taken." His bright eyes took in the room. Some cowered away from his gaze—not all appreciate a jester's japes—others gazed at him in hope.

Of course those who cowered were his special targets. "Ah, there's one who leaves naught behind," he called out, pointing to the plate. "Servants! Take theirs next. Why you'll toss it hand to hand as you depart! Lo, it was likely loaded as a cart. Beware this night, he's sure to—"

"Ho, Thome," Lord Pendrel called out quickly. He waggled a finger in warning. "I've told you, no more of those."

Thome bowed low. "As your lordship requests—no more humor." When he rose again his eyes lit on me. I waited patiently, but he stood stone still. The silence thickened. "Well, then," he said. His voice had changed drastically—was probably his normal voice. He glanced about, and his silly smile returned. "And some leave what should be taken—take thee away! Mayhap the servants drop you for a clatter and we see if you break, or merely dent."

"I have been dropped," I replied, though smiling. "See you dents or breaks?"

"A thousand cracks may mar the beauty of others—yours has fled entirely, taking with them the work of a legion of scarecrows I doubt not. Well have you come in this hour, to chase away the beasts."

I inclined my head to him, and when I looked again I saw a strange glance pass over him, as though he perceived his comments meant more than even he had first intended.

"And who else beside you then?"

"I am Thomas," he said evenly. "Her husband."

The jester's eyes went wide. "Husband indeed! How fared your heart when she took her spill and shattered her visage?"

Thomas ground his teeth. I quickly laid a hand on his arm: he was just the Fool, after all. "We were wed after that, actually."

Thome Fool's mouth gaped as he placed both hands dramatically over his heart and swooned. "Oh, true love has no one else! Bear up under all storms, all strange tongues, every need, abandonment, rejection, all evil spirits, all labors! No uglification stands in this young man's way. Why—!" He cut off abruptly, squinting. "Are you missing a leg?"

Thomas smirked. "No," he said. I think he was warming to the jokes.

The Fool went quieter. "Missing something else?" he asked—again his voice was nearly normal. When Thomas reddened, Thome's smile returned and he moved on to his next target.

Thomas and I continued to eat, a little slower now as the evening waned. Though he was supposed to bring joy—and, now and again, he did—I marveled as the Fool went around the room and left pockets of remorse. Nothing too grand, nothing to spoil the night entirely. And yet, here and there, a smile would be bitterer than another's, a sigh would carry a touch more weight.

Finally he departed, and overall the mood of the room was lighter. His Lord and Ladyship bantered a bit more.

"Forgive him, if you must," Lord Pendrel said next time he turned toward us. "Sometimes a fit overtakes him and he cuts more than he balms. He is far older than he looks—or acts, of course. He was my father's Fool as well, did you know? I inherited him along with the rest of the estate."

"Suffering sometimes brings humility though," I said gently. "I'm sure he's only doing what he feels is his work."

Lord and Lady both looked sharply at me, but after a moment uneasy smiles returned to their faces. "Of course, yes," Lord Pendrel said. He twirled his knife once. "Forgive me, I nearly asked you what suffering one so young might have experienced. But perhaps you have seen more than many."

"Enough that a few japes harm me little," I granted.

"And enough that our tower does not frighten you off."

I inclined my head.

"Do you think there is something you may do—something you may accomplish against it?" he asked. She tried not to, I could tell, and yet Lady Pendrel's ears clearly burned.

"I have twice so far come upon such things," I said. "And each time the purpose was for the Beloved to root out some sort of evil. Do you know why it is there?"

"It is not, always. Night time is when it most commonly shows—a few villagers and servants, you may have noticed, are more frightened at dusk."

"Captains, too," I murmured.

"Boris is most stout, I assure you," Lady Pendrel interjected. "Proven time and again—why, during the raids he stood head and shoulders above the rest."

His Lordship placed a hand on her arm. "Even so, dear, such a thing may unnerve anyone."

"I've no doubt Captain Boris was well-equipped to turn back invading forces," I said. "Perhaps he fears for your Lord and Ladyship, that you are suddenly outside his protection."

Lord Pendrel's eyes glittered. "Well observed, young maiden—I deem it is so."

"So the tower comes and goes. When did it first start appearing?"

They both ate steadily, as though ignoring me. I watched them, then glanced at Thomas. He shrugged, watched them along with me.

"Lordship—?"

"I feel I don't recall," he interrupted, looking up at me. His brows knit. "Harvest? Springtime?" He looked down the hall, shaking his head. "Once I began my reign, there was so much to do. And I was away, wasn't I?" He glanced over, and her Ladyship nodded mutely. Erratically. "Yes, of course I had to pay obeisance as the new Lord of Fosse. Perhaps it was already here when I came back."

From the far end of the hall a lutist strummed, a refrain I remembered from Holden—a popular song of winter. It warmed me, and I looked over at Thomas to see his contented smile. We all watched and listened for a time—he was the best I had ever heard, a voice that rang like crystal, notes plucking above the harmony to accent the lyrics. The entire hall seemed entranced—except Mahmoud, I noticed, who sat gazing darkly at the half-full trencher before him. I wondered at first why he had not finished, until I realized much of what was there was pork—a food forbidden to Moors. And he had no water to wash it down with: the Lord, in his largesse, had only wine poured. I felt a brief stab of guilt for Mahmoud. Well, if he would only accept The Beloved, I thought harshly, he could eat to his content.

As the song ended, the minstrel began another—haunting, this time, and I worried it was inappropriate. But also a few of the villagers rose, bowed to the Lord, and began to exit. I looked at him for a cue.

"You are likely tired from your journeys," he said, as though anticipating me. "You are free to go—on this night, we do not stand on ceremony. If the flurries that attended you indicate their usual, you will be spending the rest of the winter with us in Fosse."

"Are you certain, my Lord? We would hate to impose longer than necessary—we are wanderers, after all."

But he was waving his hand before I finished. "Of course not. We have ample, and to spare. No one who arrives so late ever leaves before springtime. And perhaps we might finish our conversations anon."

I rose and curtsied; Thomas bowed. A servant came near to escort us to our rooms. At first I thought we might return near our first changing room, but we were shown instead into an entirely different wing. Our servant walked swiftly but silently, his lantern lighting the way down dark halls where rushlights had not yet been lit.

We passed a dark hole where a cold wind wafted through. I paused, chilled, until he said—almost as an afterthought—"Garderobe, miss." This one apparently vented directly to the moat, rather than a pit for some unlucky servant to clean out when necessary. Still, handy to know should nature call in the dark.

A few doors further down he paused, thrusting a key into a locked and banded oaken door. He went in, and I was surprised to see a fire already glowing in the hearth. He went to the bed and removed a fire-pan that had been warming the blankets. As Thomas and I stood awkwardly by he went around the room, lighting a few rushes before opening a small wardrobe and then turning down the blankets on the bed. He paused by the door. "I am Joliff," he said. "Ask what you need of any of the servants, but mention my name and I will fulfill it. I will otherwise return for you when the cock crows. His Lordship prefers you at the dawn meal."

"He is too kind," I said. "We will be there. Thank you, Joliff."

He bowed and exited. There was clicking in the lock after he departed. I glanced around wildly, until Thomas caught my eye, smiled, and pointed: there was a second key on the bedside table.

"In case I need to use the garderobe," I said sheepishly. Then I stood there, heart hammering, waiting for Thomas to signal—anything.

He moved closer to the fire, pried his boots off. He unbuckled his sword and set it against the wall. He glanced at me over his shoulder as he undid his jacket, and I saw his fingers trembling.

It flashed to my mind in that instant that perhaps Judith had watched him in the exact same way, if not with the exact same intent—and certainly not the same implicit permission. But I assumed that permission wouldn't matter.

"Thomas," I said timidly. He paused and looked at me. "If you want, you can stay dressed for now. I mean, if it's too much like..." I saw his shoulders relax, and lowered my eyes. "I never thought—realized—until now, I guess..."

He finished quickly, and still in his nightshirt moved to the bed and slid under the blankets. I moved to the fire to remove my boots as well, and my outer skirts. Glancing over I saw him watching me intently. I moved without haste, removing each piece and hanging it over a warming rack.

Finally, when in just my shift, he said: "thank you, Rae-Anna," and lay his head down on the pillow, though he did not close his eyes. I moved to him, climbed in next to him. The cot was blissfully warm, only recently bereft of its fire-pan and with Thomas in it. He pulled me close, kissed my forehead, my nose, my lips. And then we simply held each other, man and wife, still clothed but dare I say more intimate than anything else I could have experienced.

But then, I couldn't know otherwise, could I?

Chapter 3

I awoke to the faint glow of a fire. My thoughts glittered in the darkness, arrayed before me like a jeweler's wares. Each gem held at least one flaw, I felt. Some maybe had more. They stirred, dancing before my eyes, clinking sometimes with a hollow sound. A dead sound.

"Such...misery..."

I blinked, tried to focus past the gems. The fire cast strange shadows. The hearth seemed suddenly deep and narrow, the glowing coals hissing from a great depth.

"A shame. Truly." The voice rumbled—part falling stone, part trickling water. "Are you sure you follow the true path? It is the way of the wicked that lead to destruction, and destruction looms upon you."

Light flared the same moment I felt Thomas move behind me: he had lit a lamp and now held it aloft. "There is only one who knows the end from the beginning," he said. His voice was quiet but firm.

I saw now the gems were held in scaly paws, the talons of them stirring, stirring. The light I thought was our hearth came from the dragon's eyes who seemed unperturbed by Thomas or his light. "According to whom?" he asked.

"According to Our Father," I said, bolstered a little by Thomas' confidence.

A grin curved the dragon's lips. "Of course. How precious, the faith of His fools. 'Live by faith, not by sight' He says. And yet you see for yourself now the power I have." He raised the gems a little higher, clinked them together. I glanced briefly, saw in one or two some of my memories. I saw the door to my mother and father's house slamming shut as the snow swirled. I saw myself running through the narrow streets of Holden before that, oblivious to how I used my hands—before it mattered that my left was easier to use. Talking to my friend Genevieve of our futures, so bright and buoyant back then. I tried to look up, couldn't help but notice another gem from the convent, of Thomas walking away with Judith. And yet, he did not seem as distraught as I remembered. He almost seemed eager—had it been before he knew what she would do to him? Or had he only played a part for my benefit?

The light swung, and Thomas' lantern crashed against the pile of gems. Oil and fire burst and engulfed the dragon's hands. I expected him to shout or roar as he burned, but he snickered. And then he simply clasped his hands together and extinguished the flames. "As I said," he purred, "my power is easy to see."

"You have no power over us," Thomas said. "We are The Beloved's."

The dragon's head turned as his eyes pierced us both. "Are you indeed?" He reached out a claw, and to my shock his talon scored my cheek. I recoiled, clapping a hand to the cut and I felt all the scars from the Insatiable as if they were new again.

I trembled against Thomas as the dragon's laughter rumbled. He turned languidly, his scales clinking clearer than the tainted gems, and he wormed his way into the true fire and was caught up by it. I let out a ragged sigh, went limp against Thomas.

"Is that how it always goes?" he asked.

"Often something. Always at night. Or chaotic times."

"How do we get rid of it?"

I felt a pinprick of anger. "Afraid of what I might see?"

His hand caressed my arm. "I assumed that's what we were here to do, is all."

I turned my head. "Sorry. Of course it is." I shook my head. "So far, there's always something else behind what is presented—we're here for spiritual warfare after all. We won't be able to do anything about it until we find out what the source of evil is."

"And until then, it can still hurt us in our bodies."

My hand went to my face. I felt no blood where it had cut me, but my scars were warm to the touch. "Very much so." The silence stretched. "Thomas," I murmured. "Did you see the gems? What they were?"

His arms went tight around me. "Yes."

"What did you see in them?"

His arms squeezed as he shrugged. "Oh, things I'd rather not recall, I guess," he whispered. "Why? What did you see?"

I bit my lip. "The same. Even from before the convent. Do you remember Genevieve?"

He paused. "Oh. Yeah, I do. Why?"

"Do you know what happened to her? Did she and her father work it out?"

"I don't think so. After you went away..." He went still and I twisted further to look at him.

"After that, what?"

He blinked, looked at me with soft eyes. "She... I don't want to say she needed you, but... I mean, it's not your fault, certainly, or that only you..."

"Thomas!" I said.

"She ended up marrying Lasell. He didn't treat her well—you knew he wouldn't. I think she lost her way though...or, lost sight of hope, maybe."

I turned back around, the glowing embers blurry. "It seems that happens a lot, in Holden," I said.

"I think it happens a lot everywhere, my love."

I snorted, drew a sigh. "How long did Sister Judith call you to her study before... I mean, how many times?"

Thomas went very still, and I chastened myself for asking. I don't know if I could have helped it though. As the silence continued to stretch, I pressed on. "I assume it began there? Not in town?"

"I assume you're asking about the jasper the dragon held," he said bitterly. When I held my silence this time, he continued. "I wondered." His arms unwound and he worked his way out from behind me. "Just out of curiosity, Rae-Anna, exactly how many times do I need to prove myself to you before you let this go?"

I folded my arms. "Are we supposed to be letting it go?"

He yanked his shirt on. "Sorry I'm not as articulate as you. I am still a farmer. How long before you trust me?"

"How long before you trust *me*, Thomas? I thought I was your wife—the two become one, remember? Am I not allowed to have questions about it? Can we not discuss it together?"

He gazed at me, his jaw working. "I want to," he whispered. He turned away, put his trousers on. "But that's not what you asked, was it. You saw a bauble, and worried I was lying to you about hating—*detesting*—what that woman did to me. That somehow I had to have wanted it, despite everything I've told you."

"You seem perfectly capable of denying me the same permission."

He stared at me, his gaze hardening into something I never thought I would see in him—something far worse than anything he cast at me in Aurden—and I knew I should not have said it. I was not even sure why I did. My heart was not truly in it, and yet it came out.

"Smile," he said.

I blinked, on the verge of taking back what I had said. Now I was too confused. "What?"

"Can you do it? Smile for me?"

My lip trembled at his anger. "You know—"

"You smiled at Judith before, at Sister Lucy, Mother Superior—plenty of others who hurt me, and a lot more directly. Suddenly you can't smile for me anymore?"

Tears streamed as my idiocy ran its course. "Thomas—"

"I'm broken, Rae-Anna!" he pressed relentlessly. "If I have to, I'll say sorry for hiding it so well you didn't realize—I guess in my foolishness I wanted to spare you my pain. But I can't just fix it. It can't be simply undone. Maybe if The Beloved will have healing for you, he'll have it for me, too. I don't know how, or when, or if. I have to live with it, too. Just because I don't talk about it, doesn't mean it isn't on my mind."

A rooster crowed, and as we gazed at each other there came a knock on the door. "Do you require assistance?" Joliff called gently.

Thomas turned toward the door. "Thank you, Joliff, we're making ready."

"Very good, sir."

As Joliff's padded footfalls receded, Thomas glanced at me. "I hate this," I whimpered.

He sighed, and came and sat down beside me. "Back in Holden, after you disappeared from town, I asked everywhere about you. All I ever got was silence, or signs of the cross and admonitions to mind my business. It was Genevieve, actually, who first told me you had gone to the convent. It took me another six months to convince the council just to let me deliver our tithes and surpluses. I knew, after a year, you might be beyond my reach." He took my hand in his, gently stroked the back of it. "But I swore to hold on to hope until the last possible moment. So when Sister Judith asked me to her study to discuss your progress, I was beyond eager. Either she mistook it—which I now doubt—or she knew exactly how pliable I might be. And I thought, when I saw that gem in the dragon's hand, that if only I had let you go—if I had just told myself it was already too late, that Our Father had His hand on you and you were already out of reach... Maybe we both would have been spared a lot of pain." He paused and sighed. "How can one moment change our future so much?"

I leaned over and rested my head on his shoulder. "Our enemy seeks to make the most of every chance encounter, too," I said.

Thomas hummed agreement, and we sat in silence for a time. Finally he pressed his lips against the top of my head. "Rae-Anna?" he murmured.

"Hmm?"

"I'm kind of hungry."

I chuckled, brought his hand up to my lips and kissed it. "I'm sorry I said what I said."

"I forgive you," he said. "But also I think it has something to do with this place."

I tilted my head to look at him. "Probably, huh."

His gaze went distant as he drew a deep breath. "Probably."

Breakfast with his Lordship that morning was much quieter, subdued. Her Ladyship was not present, with no comment as excuse. There was cold ham, likely remaining from the yestereve; bread rolls with honey and rich cheese; and warmed milk with roasted oats.

The hall was perhaps only half-full. I did not see Mahmoud. The Fool was there, though he only sat quietly in a corner as he ate. A tapestry here or there shuddered with the wind.

"You spent the night well?" Lord Pendrel finally asked—timidly, I thought, though his smile was firm enough.

"I've not spent many nights in castles," I admitted with a grin. "But I cannot imagine keeping one so well-appointed is easy. We slept very well. And your Lordship?"

He glanced at me, startled. "Forgive me," he said finally. "I perhaps forget your station—I am unused to such questions." He pinked, turned away a moment, forced a chuckle. It died in the thick air around us. He muttered: "perhaps it will do us well this winter to have her around." He looked at me again, his smile softer, warmer. "We did well enough, I suppose. Perhaps better than since before... Well." He waved away whatever he had been about to say.

"I understand," I said. "If I may ask, Lordship, what do you consider my station?"

"Laborer for The Beloved, of course."

"You have faith then, Lordship? Forgive me, I don't ask lightly," I hurried on. "But many perhaps serve Our Father out of fear rather than faith."

His mouth snapped shut as he studied me. He glanced sideways, shook his head. When I glanced over I saw the Fool as though he were returning to his food, saw his hand rise carefully from beneath the table where he sat.

"No apology necessary," Lord Pendrel said. His voice was easy. "As I said, I am unaccustomed to...someone of your type..." He trailed off, flustered again, and took a breath. "I admit, it can be difficult to distinguish—at least for myself. What once was faith may have turned to fear, then to desperation. Generally speaking, of course, mind you. Does Our Father despise desperation?"

"On the contrary, Lordship, I believe He is closest to those most desperate."

His face paled a moment. "Those who are desperate may not feel it," he whispered.

"Then know it, Lordship, even when you do not feel it: *Our Father is nigh unto them that are of a broken heart; and saveth such as be of a contrite spirit.*"

"Nearness is one thing," he said heavily. "Deliverance is quite another."

"You speak of the dragon."

He nodded.

"In times past, your Lordship, the history of a place we are called to serve helps us free it from whatever evil is befalling it."

"Castle Fosse is very old," he said with a smirk. "That may take some time."

"All winter?" I asked with a grin.

He raised his cup in salute. "Of course. Perhaps you might visit the archives for the deeper history, and I'll save myself for more recent events."

"Of course, Lordship," I said, bowing my head. I looked over to see Thomas had likewise finished, and a servant stood behind us. "I look forward to wintering at your table, Lordship—you have outdone yourself."

He returned to his plate while the servant showed us out of the hall. Joliff waited just outside the door, looked at our escort patiently.

"His Lordship wishes them to see the archives," he said quietly.

I was looking at Joliff, saw the fear flash quickly through his eyes. Before I could ask, his mouth hardened and he shooed away the other servant. He turned with a swirl of his tunic and strode purposefully down the hall.

There was a brief rattle beside me, and I saw Thomas' hand just below his sword hilt. "What do you think it means?" I whispered as we hurried to keep up with Joliff.

Thomas began to shake his head, startled as a door next to us burst open. His sword was halfway out before we recognized the Fool.

"Joliff!" the Fool cried. Joliff stuttered to a stop, turned, and managed to put on a patient smile. Thome made a show of gasping for air before finally straightening and striking a pose that—after only seeing it once or twice—I immediately knew to be Lord Pendrel's.

Joliff had likely seen it countless times and stood unimpressed. "Yes, Fool?"

Thome sagged, leaving off the pose. "There was a misunderstanding," he said. "I fear Fabien thought his Lordship meant for you to archive our guests." He rolled his eyes with a dramatic patient sigh.

Joliff reddened just enough, hesitated to glance our way enough, that I wondered if there had indeed been such a misunderstanding. I felt rather than saw Thomas shift, and knew he gripped his sword a little tighter.

"I am sure Fabien thought no such thing," Joliff said with a smile. "Now, how may I help you?"

"I'll take them," he offered quickly.

Joliff paled, and I knew he took insult. "Sometimes, Fool, you go too—"

"Oh, hillocks! Now I've gone and been misunderstood!" The Fool capered a moment, and with a flourish of his hands suddenly presented a rose—badly wilted—to Joliff. "Pax?" he asked, and the bloom toppled sideways and broke from its stem.

As we all stared at the petals splattered on the floor, Joliff asked drily: "Are you sure you can find the way?"

Thome affected the Lord's pose again. "Better than my own father!"

Joliff glanced at us. "Of that, I've no doubt."

"Joliff," Thomas began, glancing worriedly at the Fool.

Joliff raised a hand. "He's mostly harmless," he said. The Fool simply kept up his pose. Joliff leaned in close. "And anyway, he would never miss a meal—not even for a prank."

Before we could say anything, Joliff walked off and quickly turned down a corridor. We both looked at the Fool, who only stared imperiously at us.

Then he dashed off down the hall and disappeared from sight. Thomas took one step forward, then whirled to face me.

"Um..."

I shrugged and clasped my hands in front of me to wait. "Not like we can't find the hall when the next meal comes along," I said.

"I'm re-thinking your comment about how well Lord Pendrel keeps his..."

"His keep?"

"His halls, I was going to say." Thomas crossed his arms and leaned back against the wall. "Are we sure we trust this Fool?"

"We trust Our Father," I said automatically. I glanced at him, lowering my eyes when his gaze flashed. "I understand what you mean. Would you like to chase after him?" I asked, smiling.

Thomas' smile slowly fell, and he looked down the hall. "Come with me," he said.

"Anywhere," I replied with a hint of mischief.

Thomas glowered playfully at me over his shoulder. "We really need to work on your timing," he said. I came up closer behind him, reaching forward to touch his hand. His fingers clasped mine and we strolled down the halls.

Thomas took a few different turns, then opened a door to a stairwell. I glanced at him—it was poorly lit, and we still had no sign of the Fool. "Where are we going?" I asked.

"Oh, I thought you knew too. We're going to the archives, I think."

"Thomas, how would you know that?"

"Well," he said, starting down the steps ahead of me with his hand on his sword, "I guess I trust Our Father."

I picked up my skirts and followed him. We exited the bottom, and Thomas turned left and continued down he hall. Another right, and then he stopped in front of a set of double doors. A small brass placard nailed to the right side said: "Archives."

Thomas shrugged and pushed on the door, just as the opposite door opened outward and the Fool stopped short. He stared at us, cheeks sucked in.

"About time," he said, though I thought perhaps he was more surprised than he let on. "I thought I would have to come find you." He ushered us in, saying: "Leave it to Joliff to ruin a perfectly good joke."

"He didn't tell us where it was," Thomas said simply.

The Fool stopped, and his voice went cold. "Did he not?"

I turned to look at him, and thought for the briefest moment I saw a many-hued glint in his eye. But then it was gone as he swept his fingers in front of his face. "Mysterious!" he mocked. He strode past us. "The archivist is this way. But be warned," he called over his shoulder. "He'll steal the clothes off your back if he doesn't like you. And he loves to collect memories as though they were jewels."

Chapter 4

"Do you think he meant that?" Thomas hissed as we followed slowly behind the Fool. We wandered among stacks of shelves and rows of tables, covered in books and scrolls with bare circles where candles might stand.

"He means a lot of things," I said calmly. "This castle seems sometimes full of knowledge." I gave Thomas a meaningful glance.

He shrugged. "But I thought my knowledge came from Our Father."

He sounded almost hurt, and I gripped his arm. "I'm not saying it didn't. Perhaps Our Father speaks through Fools as well as though brave men."

When Thomas looked at me, I felt the fire flicker inside—felt at the same moment that Thomas said: "*But God hath chosen the foolish things of the world to confound the wise.*"

I smiled at him. "Almost makes you not want to be too smart, doesn't it?"

"Don't say that to the Archivist," Thomas replied.

Ahead of us, the Fool started whispering nonsense as though to someone. He seemed to get quite angry with whoever it was, and finally broke off with a raised hand. "Here," he said in normal tones, then bellowed: "Favish!"

The call echoed around the room, and a moment later there came a flutter of padded footfalls. A portly man rounded a shelf, eyes glaring. "Yes, thank you, *Piter*. I know you have no use for this place, so begone please."

Rather than appearing hurt, or making some jibe, the Fool turned silently on his heel and left. I raised an eyebrow at Thomas as I turned back, then looked at the Archivist. He was clad in striped silks, wore soft slippers, and what was left of his hair was a raven-black. He had, I suddenly noticed, a left eye gone pale—his remaining blue eye was clear and glittered as he studied me as frankly as I realized I was studying him.

"Sometimes he relishes that role as Thome Fool a little too much." He wagged his head and sighed. "What brings you here, then?" he asked. His voice was deep but pleasant. I trusted him.

"His Lordship said we might learn more of the older history of Castle Fosse here, and he might fill us in with more recent details later," I said.

He glanced between us. "You are also archivists?"

I could tell by his tone he hoped for kindred spirits, so I smiled to soften the blow. "I'm afraid not. We go where Our Father's Sacred Fire sends us—and, so far, histories have helped us address the issues we find where He sends us."

His hopeful smile dimmed as he nodded. "The child?" he asked.

I looked at Thomas, then back. "I'm not sure what you mean. Which child?"

"I assumed you were here for the tower?"

"Yes, but..." I faltered, feeling around the strange sense of trust I had felt. It was still there, still seemed solid. "His Lordship indicated..."

"Others have seen a dragon," Thomas said, stepping forward. "Is there nothing in your archives about that?"

The Archivist cocked his head a moment, then shook it. "I see what you mean," he said sadly. "It's easy, sometimes, to feel useless—documenting, no matter how meticulously, a series of events only *after* it's too late to change them. To be a good archivist is often to see the world from the past."

"Until today," I said. "If we find the key to a brighter future for Castle Fosse through some clue that you have so meticulously logged and stored."

He spread his hands. "And where would you start?" he asked of the dizzying array of records surrounding us.

"Let's start with the child," I said. "Do you mind if we sit?"

"Oh, please do!" He hurriedly cleared some chairs and we all sat down. "Yes, the child. First sighted—" He squinted upward. "Third day of Harvest last year, just past noon, by the chandler. Or so my reports indicate."

"Lady Pendrel said no one saw her but they two," I said.

He gave a thin smile. "There is much whispered behind the back of the Lords by their servants," he said. "My duty is to record, and show those records to his Lordship—or Ladyship—when asked." He emphasized the last, laying a finger alongside this nose.

"They suffer alone—or believe they do," I said. He held his silence as it occurred to me that was true of many people. I let it go. "Who is she?"

His eyes flashed. "You assume she is someone we would recognize?"

I cocked my head. "Is she?"

He shifted uncomfortably. "None have seen her closely enough to identify her. Just a slip of a thing, thin hair. A waif." He waved his hand as if she were unimportant—or would be if she were of flesh and bone.

"In Holden, there was once a young boy whose hair was never cut. Many times I mistook him for a young girl..."

"No, this one is definitely a girl."

"How do you know?" I pressed. I smiled as he fidgeted. "Master Archivist, we cannot help if we are not told the truth."

"Truth." He heaved a sigh and glanced around the room. "Do you know the job of an archivist? You see this room—these shelves and tables packed with scrolls and books, the history of this realm. That's why you're here. Documented, tallied, and curated by—how did you call me? Master Archivist?" He snorted and shook his head. "There are few with the title of 'Master.' Each one would be reckoned as truest in their work—yes? A master stonemason wrestles art from stone. No finer foundation laid, no walls more plumb. Master carpenters build the truest lengths, the surest joints, the most accurate carvings. When one might think of the truest form of something—that is what the Master Craftsman promises. And what is my craft? To preserve truth? What truth?"

"Of history, I would say."

He inspected my face. "And I would say the true history of you was...an attack of some kind? To bear scars like that?"

"I was assailed, yes, but not by mere mortal men," I allowed.

"So. You were attacked, your face was marred. It healed eventually, but not fully, and you carry the scars. Is that the truth?"

I glanced at Thomas and nodded. "Yes," I said uncertainly.

"And that was the entirety of the experience? Just as I laid it out?"

I remembered the attack, the fog afterward, the strange journey into darkness and back. Tabitha's ministrations and what healing it worked in both mind and body—and what healing it could not bring. All the emotions around how Thomas would react. I shook my head.

"Of course it isn't. No list of facts that could be penned will ever convey the truth of an event." He shook his head, gazing off into the vast collections of books around him. "If you want the truth," he continued, his voice low, "do not call me Master; I am Favish. And I know it is a girl because her appearance is too akin to the mistress Pendrel."

At the name his lips clamped shut and he bowed his head. For a time the only sound was the sputtering of candles, and of our breathing.

"I'm sorry," I whispered finally. "We hadn't heard."

Favish wiped his eyes and looked up. "No," he said huskily. "I imagine you didn't. The grief is still too near for too many." A ghost of a smile crossed his lips. "Including me."

"Tell us about her," I said.

"The truth?" he asked wryly.

"Perhaps, that which tells you of a certainty that the girl on the tower is her."

He nodded. "Indeed—well spoken. She was...the light of this castle. How do some say it? That someone brightens a room? Call me a fool if you wish, but I can promise more than once the candles truly dimmed when she entered. Smart, kind, generous in words and deeds—obedient, but not subservient. Even so young, there were many who trembled for the poor lordling who would marry her." He laughed shortly. "Oh, she would do him no harm. But we all knew—barring accident—she would run the manor far better than any lord this country has ever produced. Nothing against his

Lordship, of course."

"Of course."

"As fine a lord as his father, Lord Pendrel is. And the Lady! Only from those two could such delightful offspring come."

"And yet..."

He drew a deep sigh. "And yet. She fell, from that very keep."

I raised my eyebrows. "How?"

He shrugged, his hands spread. "She was alone, as near as we can tell. Lord Pendrel's inquisitor conducted quite the thorough investigation."

"I can imagine," I said.

"Huh. Everyone was accounted for—everyone. It was concluded she had been up there alone, perhaps thought to peer through the crenelation, and overbalanced." He shook his head.

"You disagree."

"Her curiosity was never so careless."

"She was murdered?"

He sniffed, pulled himself upright and looked at his books. "Our records state the Mistress Pendrel climbed the tower to enjoy a view of the countryside, peered through the ramparts, and perhaps overbalanced or was struck by an errant gust of wind." He shrugged miserably. "Or maybe she saw a mouse or a bird in distress and, in trying to reach it, fell to her death against the stones."

I glanced at Thomas. "And then she began appearing atop the tower—or, a ghost who appears to be Mistress Pendrel did." I took a careful breath. "The pagans would say a ghost appears because justice is wanting."

He peered at me. "You disagree?"

"The Holy Word does not speak much about ghosts," I said, "except one who tried to call one up and was condemned for it."

"Perhaps someone has succeeded—or does succeed—in calling her up, then."

"Who might do that?"

He glanced between Thomas and myself, then at the door. But when he looked back, he was resolutely silent.

I decided to move on—that might become clearer later. "What of the tower and the dragon?"

"Ah. That may take a bit more telling."

"Why?"

"That dragon has ancient ties to Castle Fosse—far before all our times. The stories were old when my predecessor was a boy. Almost every account I've read—and I've gone through most—contain some reference or other, back to the founding."

I peered at Thomas. *Sounds like Aurden.* I could tell by his glance he thought the same. "Lord Pendrel said he thought the tower, though, appeared when he was gone to swear fealty."

Favish grinned. "Old memories have ways of playing tricks on us, I think. Perhaps he meant that was when it first appeared under his reign."

"Either way, he seemed uncertain. In all those references, is there mention of why the dragon is here? What it is?"

Favish glanced aside. "So many are so vague—or written as though the reader already knows about it. Though..." His brows drew down. "Perhaps his Lordship has one point: I cannot say it was *seen*. Because I never truly thought about it until his ascension. Isn't that odd? And yet when you first asked..." He waved his hand in front of his face as though clearing a mist.

"As though you suddenly realized you already knew it?" *Too much like Aurden.*

But he glanced hard at me. "Not quite. As I said, the dragon is an established peculiarity of Castle Fosse—you may ask anyone. And so when it appeared—truly appeared—it was comfortable. As though being told an old friend is at home, and you take it for granted even if you haven't got eyes on him. But when you do, you say 'well of course, he was here all along.'"

"I see." I looked at Thomas for a time, trying to gauge his thoughts. "Since the dragon and the tower are linked," I said slowly, "perhaps we'll start there. Would you mind directing us to whatever references you have? Starting with the oldest, I would say."

He nodded. "I will bring them to you."

As Favish departed into the stacks of shelves, Thomas moved a little closer. He drew a candle near, massaged my back as we bent over the table to wait. I was learning to appreciate every small gesture Thomas offered. "What do you think happened to Mistress Pendrel?" I murmured.

He shrugged, while his hand never stopped moving. "That might be something to ask his Lordship. He would know the details of the investigation better."

"Do you think he would meet with you?"

Thomas flashed me a grin. "I think he would be happy to meet with you, speaker for The Beloved."

"Laborer," I corrected, elbowing him. "But there might still be things he would keep from me—either for fear of appearing too tender, or thinking he protects me from harsh realities."

"I'll see if he will."

Thomas' hand dropped away as Favish returned with the first handful of scrolls, and a little page of scribbled notes. "To help you find the references a little faster," he explained. He showed me the notes and how to decipher them. "If I may—there will be much to read, and I may forget, but..." He grinned, shaking his head. "Forgive me, I rattle on. If I need to leave, I must ask you to leave as well. I keep this room locked when I am away." He drew out a key on a cord around his neck to show us. "To prevent tampering, you understand. And..." He paused, tucked it away again as his face darkened briefly. "And to prevent foolish jokes."

I cocked an eyebrow at Thomas as Favish left us to it as he returned to his shelves. "I wonder if Thome Fool is as harmless as his station says he should be," I mused.

Thomas shrugged, and we returned to the scrolls. What I came to delight in about Favish is that he never exaggerated or embellished. The early references were nearly useless, and all spoke of the dragon as though taken for granted—as though green grass, blue skies, and black dragons were all normal parts of our world. But also true to his word—and, I admit, it took a while to notice—none of them actually referenced seeing the dragon.

"Some of these almost make me think it was never real, just something the first tenants blamed," I said after the fifth scroll went back into the row.

"Like a superstition," Thomas agreed. "Anything that couldn't be explained, *the dragon did it,*" he added with a dramatic flair.

I chuckled. "Something like that." My grin faded as I looked over the scrolls, running through them again in my mind. "Was it always at night?"

Thomas considered. "If you read them to me right, I think so."

We opened the next scroll, and I checked Favish's notes. "This one should be more detailed. Let's see..." I found the passage, but before I began reading where he indicated I noticed a line further up. *Twice they assailed the keep, and the third time they gained the second floor. The heir was taken, later found slain. No vengeance could be sought, no justice attained. For oaths made in haste are often a slow acid, and what they devour none can foresee. Beware thy words!*

"What is that talking about?" Thomas asked. "And where's the part about the dragon?"

I shook my head. "Favish might know. The dragon is further down. 'Seek not the gleam in the dragon's eye, for what it covets it protects. Many are those whose bodies litter that dark mount, whose lives were spent in upward toil, cast again and again against those slopes which should have been abandoned. Why waste thyself? *Drink waters out of thine own cistern, and running waters out of thine own well.*'" I paused, brow furrowed. "That last part was from the Holy Words," I said. I read further, silently. "That's all of it. It begins to recount another event entirely from there." I set the scroll down and we looked at each other. "That is coming close to being specific."

"The first to sound like the dragon is an actual thing, too," he agreed.

"Given our experience with the dragon, it would mean what? Don't seek your memories?"

"Or the memories of another."

"Is that why Lord Pendrel seemed so vague on when the dragon appeared? Is it taking his memories?"

Thomas chewed his lip. "I don't see how that would work. I still have the memories we saw in it. Don't you?"

I sat back and rubbed my eyes. "Yes, I guess I do."

Thomas was silent for a moment, then whispered my name. I looked at him, saw a hint of shame in his eyes. "Oh no, I don't mean it that way. I'm just a little tired from the reading I guess. But you're right, there has to be more to it. Something else to bring up with Lord Pendrel if you get the chance. Oh, Favish!" I said as he appeared, now with a stack of books. I held up the scroll and recounted the story of the kidnapped and slain heir. "What is it talking about there?"

He sat heavily. "That would have been...four sires ago? Five. It was the fourth heir that was taken—supposed to be fourth. Lord Rotel Pendrel made an oath to help Lord Karnisson against an invading force. Swore that if he failed, the punishment would be laid on his son." Favish paused and raised his eyes heavenward. "Sounded noble, I suppose. Anyway, Karnisson was not accurate in his counting of his enemy. Rotel upheld his part as best he could, nearly destroyed his army in the process, but defeat was inevitable. Karnisson refused to see it, and demanded his price. Rotel refused, and Karnisson attacked. Of course, he had stayed mostly inside his keep during the invasion, so his knights were still strong. Lord Rotel defended as best he could but they were exhausted. His eldest was taken, as you read. The second gained the throne—a fine lad, for what he was. But I think perhaps the king felt he was still second-best. There was a shadow cast against Fosse that day that I would daresay has never lifted."

"A weaker heir, weaker offspring—or so it is looked at," Thomas said quickly as Favish's eyes flashed. "I'm not saying anything against his Lordship."

Favish relaxed. "Yes. Of course."

"And so the following lines, about seeking not the gleam of the dragon's eye—"

"Pride, perhaps? Some have said Rotel's downfall was his pride, to make such an oath without having seen the opposing forces himself."

Thomas and I glanced at each other. "Would memories have anything to do with it?" Thomas asked.

Favish considered, but slowly shook his head. "Not that I recall...unless you think the dragon takes the memories from us?" he asked, suddenly alarmed.

"Not take them, no," I said quickly. "At least, it doesn't seem so.

But perhaps we'll find more as we read."

Wary, but apparently trusting, Favish left again. "I wonder how many he has in here," I mused, staring at the two piles before us. "And how much outside of the references to dragons we should read."

Thomas chewed his lip. "This would go faster if I could read too," he muttered.

I smiled. "Well, I could teach you. Writing too, if you want."

He looked around at all the books, shelf upon shelf, then finally at me. "I might like that," he said. "Sitting here among all this, all the history here... But then thinking of what you've already accomplished. I keep feeling like someone should write it all down."

"Maybe you could, to practice."

He shook his head. "So far this is much more your story than mine. I guess I could eventually fill in some details, if it becomes important."

"If I have time, I suppose," I said. "I feel like we're going to be far too busy right now, though."

He shrugged. "We might wait forever for enough time."

I smiled, then. I can't help but laugh now—with only a little bitterness—at how true his words would become. Our Father forgive us for the times we waste not doing what we should, and for granting us more time when we do not deserve it.

Forgive me for spoiling it, but we did teach Thomas to write that winter. And I've asked him now to write the next chapters, since it was he who alone gained an audience with Lord Pendrel the next day.

And, truth be told, there is much to write and I feel that time is growing shorter.

Chapter 5

THOMAS

We were up late the next morning. After reading and searching through the books until nearly supper, we were exhausted. Lord Pendrel was kind to us at the evening meal—I'm not sure who told him, but he seemed to know. At least he didn't barrage us with questions, and waited patiently if our minds were fuzzy with thinking. I say 'we' but Rae-Anna seemed sharp as ever, though she had done all of the reading. I comforted myself by saying I did all the thinking. Even though I didn't.

By the end of the meal—smaller than the first night, but still ample—I had managed to ask him if he and I could speak privately at some point. He had agreed, which was why Joliff came to wake us the next morning and tell me his Lordship was to ride out later that day and that I should join him.

Rae-Anna still had that patient look to her eyes. At least it was only patience today. I think she didn't realize that her annoyance showed through sometimes, even if it didn't also come out in her words. She was trying. As was I. I knew I was, anyway. I could tell she sometimes didn't believe me.

But, that morning, tired as I was, even the patient look felt like too much. Did she expect me to take her right then? Joliff waiting outside for a response? Lord Pendrel probably waiting for us to break our fast?

Forgive me that I was unkind to her in that moment. Everything was still raw and ragged, at least to me. She didn't know how often Sister Judith popped into my vision—probably wouldn't have understood if I tried to tell her. Especially after the dragon showed us those memories. But too often, it would be as though Rae-Anna's face—so precious to me for so long—looked too much like Judith. I could not shake it. And when I saw it, everything else came flooding back too. And my stomach would roll over inside me, and I would have to look away before some unintended emotion played across my face.

I wanted to tell her. Well, let's say I wished she knew. I couldn't tell her, didn't know how to begin. I just hoped it would eventually go away. Before her patient looks angered me so much that I did something I would regret.

So that morning I just dressed, and was silent—very intentionally silent. We both knew. Usually I gave her some token that I was not that angry, especially not at her. I didn't do it that morning though. Not even a look. I dressed, stomped my feet into my boots, and went out the door.

Joliff stood waiting, also silent. He looked at me only once, cocked an eyebrow as though he understood (I don't think he actually did), and gave me the smallest of sympathetic smiles. And when Rae-Anna exited, I still didn't look at her. I just couldn't see her disappointment again, and I swallowed against everything that wanted to come out.

By the time we made it back to the Hall, we had ignored each other enough to pretend again that nothing had happened. I took the seat next to Lord Pendrel this time.

"It often happens this way," he said to me, gesturing to the narrow windows high up on the wall. "Winter: it comes in biting and clawing, then settles down once we've respected it."

I smiled. "Perhaps that's what we in Holden do wrong," I said. "We forget to respect it, and it bites and claws until Spring finally chases it away for us."

Lord and Lady Pendrel both chuckled, and when I glanced over I saw even Rae-Anna seemed to appreciate the humor. "Still, it cannot be worse than the far north," Lord Pendrel continued. "My father and I had one occasion to go that way, and one would think the winter solstice had come to stay into even the fourth month."

"A hardy people come from those regions," Rae-Anna mentioned.

Lord Pendrel glanced at her in surprise. "Have you been there? I forget how much you must travel."

She smiled, her radiance undimmed by the scars. Another thing I should have told her every time I could, and somehow forgot. "No, though some came to the convent—and I heard their language."

Lady Pendrel shuddered as his Lordship nodded sagely. "It is ungracious, their speech," he said. "And direct, from what little I heard translated. No room for subtlety or nuance." He shook his head sadly. "I fear it will be their undoing."

"How so?" I asked. I never thought language could be someone's undoing.

Lord Pendrel lowered his voice. "Well, courts demand it," he said. "We cannot offend sensibilities, but some topics require it. Or situations. In those cases, one must be subtle. But if one possesses not the language—the means—to be subtle..." He trailed off with a regretful frown. "The civilized world knows this, and can accommodate it.

Despite many of our differences, we can at least sit at the same table. The men from the North too often cannot, and will never benefit from our civilization."

"Do you perceive then, your Lordship, that The Beloved is not for everyone?" Rae-Anna asked. I glanced at her, recognizing the tone. I only hoped she wouldn't anger his Lordship before I had a chance to ride with him.

"Not of The Beloved's will, of course," Lord Pendrel replied. "But if a race of people so build their civilization as to reject him..."

"And if they receive him?" she pressed. "Must they still change their language to join your courts?"

"Speaking of subtlety," I muttered into my cup of warmed milk. I tasted it, and frowned. "This is wonderful," I said—blurted, I guess. It surprised me. "What's in it?"

Lord Pendrel's eyes softened as he grinned. "My wife's making," he said. "Her Ladyship is partial to cinnamon. And if we roast and crumble barley into it as well, it carries even a dash of cinnamon throughout the cup."

"I'm very pleased you like it," her Ladyship said.

We ate in silence for a little longer before his Lordship looked up again. "You have not said so, but I take it you are comfortable riding? I know you did not come here by horse."

I nodded. "Yes. At least, I've been on horseback. Not a warhorse or anything."

Lord Pendrel smiled. "It will not be that kind of ride, do not worry. Betimes I enjoy a ramble through the countryside."

"If I may ask, your Lordship: your...what besets this castle. It does not harass you in the daytime?"

"Ah, subtlety. But no, it does not." He turned as her Ladyship's hand rested on his arm. "Well it has not, and not for lack of opportunity, my love. Do Our Beloved's Laborers perceive any threat?"

I turned to look at Rae-Anna as she smiled gently. "That is not always my gift, Lordship," she said. "But no."

"Well, that's settled. I lay no responsibility on you if your guess goes amiss, lady, but I am heartened by it nonetheless."

Rae-Anna inclined her head, but as she turned back to her plate she paused and glanced at me. She pitched her voice for me alone. "You should take Mahmoud," she said.

I cocked my head. "He is a better swordsman than I am," I agreed. "But you just said—"

"Not for his sword, Thomas."

I glanced at Lord Pendrel, who remained occupied by her Ladyship. "Are you sure? If he's uncomfortable with Northmen..." I trailed off as Rae-Anna looked at me. I do believe Our Father gifted women with eyes to get a man's attention when He Himself could not. I held her gaze for a moment longer. At that point I just wanted to enjoy myself with what I could. And then I gave her the slightest smile, and saw the realization dawn in those most precious of soul-jewels. She reddened only slightly as she wrinkled her nose at me.

I really needed to sort through the mess in my head, to be the sort of husband she wanted, and stop...

Just like that, her visage took on the form of Judith. I looked away quickly as though turning to his Lordship, finding her arm with my hand and giving her a slight squeeze. "You Lordship, if I can impose: would it be possible to bring Mahmoud with us? He has become a close companion in our travels already."

"The Moor?" Lord Pendrel asked, his voice drained of most of its warmth. He hesitated. "Unless, in your travels, he has become..."

I glanced down the hall, noticing just then that Mahmoud had entered quietly and sat separately. The rest of that table, too, had those people most courts would deem inappropriate. I'm sure his Lordship considered it generous that they sat there at all. The Seed—Rae-Anna called it the Fire, but I felt a Seed—sprouted in me.

"He is not yet, Lordship," I said. "Yet, aren't we supposed to *Go out into the highways and hedges, and compel them to come in, that Our Father's house may be filled?"*

Lord Pendrel's face twitched between annoyance and grudging acceptance. "Yes, of course. But—"

"But do we not suffer temptation and trials by too close association with evil?" Lady Pendrel piped up. "Does it not also say 'Abstain from all appearance of evil, that it may go well with you?'"

The Seed grew, sending out lush broad leaves. "It does, your Ladyship—though, those are two separate passages and shouldn't be haphazardly joined. For it also says *'not to company with fornicators: yet not altogether with the fornicators of this world; for then must ye needs go out of the world.'* And *'How then shall they call on him in whom they have not believed? and how shall they believe in him of whom they have not heard? and how shall they hear without a preacher?'"*

Lord Pendrel held up his hand. "Enough." He shook his head at the both of us, though he grinned. "If you work as hard at convincing the Moor, he'll be wed to The Beloved ere our ride ends."

"I'm sorry if I made too bold, your Lordship." Though, with Rae-Anna's hand trembling against my arm, and the marriage of her Fire to my Seed as the sun warms a crop, I did not actually regret it.

"Sometimes the direct assault wins the day," he said. "But come! Let us ride before we argue the Holy Word until the midday meal."

In the flurry that followed as servants made us all ready, I was able to pause briefly with Rae-Anna. I breathed deep, with my eyes closed, and when I opened them looked only into her eyes. Those, of all of her, held nothing of Sister Judith in them.

"I never heard you speak so," she said.

"Maybe I've been around you long enough, finally," I said.

"Or you've had Our Father's Sacred Fire long enough—"

I shook my head. "I told you, I don't have that. I think He came as fire the first time so I would know what it was, but for me He is a Seed inside, giving me life and strength. And the Holy Words like He gives you."

"Oh. Should we..." She took half a step back. "Is that okay? Doesn't fire—I mean, I don't want to read too much into it, but..."

I laughed. "No, you won't burn my crops. Plants need the sun, after all."

She leaned closer. I kissed the top of her head, catching it with my hand to make sure she wouldn't step away too soon. "I love you, Rae-Anna," I whispered into her hair. "We will figure this out, somehow." I rested my cheek, now, glancing down the hall to see Mahmoud's eyes glittering at me as a servant waited on him. "Surely with Our Father's help with everything else..." I trailed off as Mahmoud nodded the servant away and stood. "Are you sure we should have asked Mahmoud to ride with his Lordship and I?"

She looked up at me, then at him. Her hand rested against my chest. "You did say *compel them to come in*," she said.

"Are you sure whatever is going to happen out there will compel him?"

Her eyes searched mine. "Are *you* sure?"

I sighed. "No. At least, whatever happens won't be the only step. Just one of them."

But as we rode through the broad valley, I began to wonder if that step would even happen. The sky was cloudless, the sun bright. Though most of the field lay fallow, and the air was crisp, it felt more the end of winter than just the beginning. I could see why Lord

Pendrel wanted to ride—though, not why he agreed to let me ride with him.

We began to circle back toward the castle, and the Seed inside me cracked once more. I nudged the gentle bay he had given me, and rode up beside him. "Your Lordship," I said quietly. "I had thought to talk to you about—"

He glanced sharply at me, but I saw his fortifications quickly fall. "You are right, master Thomas," he said. With a click, he nudged his roan stallion westward again. His attendants—and Mahmoud, trailing us—followed without question. "Let us ride a little further," he murmured to me. "There's a particular vantage point I am fond of. We've even made a small camp there, and I believe our cook has made us a luncheon." He glanced meaningfully at one of the servants' bulging saddlebags.

"Thank you, Lordship," I replied with a grin.

We passed between the farms, riding clear of the fields laying ready for spring. We came upon a winding path, through groves and angling generally for the southern mountains. The path continued between great slabs of stone and rocky hills, only wide enough for perhaps two horses, if the outer horse didn't mind a fall sometimes on their left side. But the path was well made, and well kept, and after entering another thick stand of pines opened wide on a natural shelf. I could already see through the trunks, that we were now high above Castle Fosse.

The attendants stopped without command and began making a small camp. The remains of a fire were clear, as well as several lean-tos. We looped the reins around some branches and Lord Pendrel gestured me to follow him. As I did, I glanced at Mahmoud, gesturing him to come but not too close. He glanced heavenward briefly, but followed anyway.

We ducked through a final few low-hanging branches before stepping out onto a rock edge, nearly like a parapet. I saw some work with tools done to the one end, so they had probably leveled it a little. Below us the mountains fell away and the river glittered as it circled the castle. It was easier from up here to understand how the fields had been planted, that they took advantage of those areas with the most sunlight. With a winter's sun, and probably some days barely peeking over the mountains, the shadows would stretch far.

I looked up, and Lord Pendrel was watching me with an approving glint in his eye. "You said your family had farmed," he observed.

"Yes, Lordship."

"Though you wear a sword, your mind goes first to seed and harvest, not to defenses."

I hadn't thought of it. "Yes, Lordship," I repeated.

He gazed downward, and I could tell he was looking at the castle. "Then there are the people, the trades needed to support those people—you have not heard of Lourendes, I can only imagine." I shook my head. "Fascinating man. He determined how many people a lord needed to support various trades. How many soldiers and farmers per blacksmith, how many for cobblers, coopers, bakers, leatherworkers, weavers..."

"To support them?" I asked. "I thought they supported the people."

"That is part of Lourendes' genius. How often did your family go into town to purchase their goods? Or trade for them, however you achieved it."

I shrugged. "Maybe once a year. Father fixed most things on his own..." I trailed off, the truth dawning on me.

Lord Pendrel nodded. "I must say, Thomas, you are very clever. Not like...well. Some. Most farmers do most of their own work.

Probably your mother mended most of your clothes, you would do many repairs to your own footwear—"

"Or not wear it during the summer months," I added with a smile.

"Or not wear them. And a cobbler cannot pay for his food on one farmer's needs, or even fifty."

"That's why vendors have to apply to the lord before opening a shop," I said.

"One of the many tedious things we Lords keep our thumbs on. In many places—much larger than this—the Guilds serve for that. Here, I alone am responsible for the people, the trades, often times the prices. Merchants, too," he continued with a half-glance toward Mahmoud. "Too many, and I must find a way to support those permanently here until they've moved on. Too few...well, there's not much to do there. Sometimes we must all go without."

I looked at him with growing respect. And I wondered how much our mayor in Holden did the same. "You handle it very well, your Lordship," I said.

His eyes went dark for a brief moment. "I was not looking for your approval," he said. I lowered my eyes; I was still a common man to him. He sighed. "Well, we all have our demesnes to oversee. I have Fosse and its environs, you have your wife Rae-Anna, and the task given to you by Our Father."

Now I looked at the castle, wondering what Rae-Anna was up to. She had mentioned going to the Archives again. "I fear I am not doing so well a job," I muttered.

"I am certain it's not the life you were brought up for," Lord Pendrel offered.

I thought of our journeys so far, but also—of course—about the events at the convent. No man was brought up for that kind of life. I had been trapped in Holden, trapped in Aurden, by evil forces while my wife had done the work of defeating it. No, it was not how I was raised. And it made the sword by my side even more of a joke. I had not used it against Judith—Rae-Anna and her Fire had handled that. I had not used it against Mr. Messick—again, Rae-Anna. Why did I even pursue her? Why had I sought her out so ardently in Holden, and in the convent? How much easier to have let her go, to stay on my father's farm?

"Do you think, Lordship, that one innocent decision can ruin the rest of a man's life?"

He was silent, and when I looked over I saw him trembling slightly before he spoke. "Do you think, Master Thomas, there is such a thing as an innocent decision?"

I tried to answer, but nothing came out. The Seed in me was hard and shriveled. I had pursued Rae-Anna out of childish lusts. How was it St. Paul said it? When I became a man I put away childish things. Well, when *he* did; I never became a man, and I coveted Rae-Anna like some shiny bauble. And in pursuing her I had fallen into Judith's trap. As much as I wanted to blame only her—and she had a fair share—she had only used my existing sin and magnified it for her own ends. I could have walked away. When Rae-Anna disappeared from Holden's streets, I could have left it alone. Sought a farmer's wife. Now...

Lord Pendrel gasped, and I looked up. The dragon soared over the castle, glittering eyes searching.

"He's early," Pendrel cried. "He has never come so early! Never—except..." His eyes went wide as he frantically searched.

We both saw it at the same time: a young girl on the tower's peak, playing, oblivious to the malevolent force above her. She seemed to be balancing along the crenellating, clambering over the jagged teeth of the tower.

"What is she—?" He broke off, dashing back toward camp. "To horse!" he shouted. "My daughter—my daughter is in peril!"

I ran with him, bewildered. "Lordship!" I called out. "She is already gone, isn't she—?"

He whirled on me, eyes blazing. "You say I cannot protect my daughter?" He turned again and leaped onto his horse. His hooves ripped up great chunks of earth as he tore off down the trail, his Lordship still shouting.

I tried to follow, but my gentle horse was no match for his stallion. When I finally exited the trees into the fields, the dragon was gone and Lord Pendrel was hunched over in the grass weeping.

Chapter 6

THOMAS

"Lordship?" I asked gently.

He did not answer, and in the silence I heard the rest of his entourage arriving behind me. They gathered but said nothing. As I looked at each of them, I could tell they did not judge him. In some, it looked to me like they weren't surprised, either. Mahmoud alone was turned a little away, and did not watch.

I dismounted and knelt next to Lord Pendrel. "My lord, when we met with the Archivist, he said no one had seen the child close enough to know who she was. But now, you seem to know exactly who it is, and why she is there."

Lord Pendrel tightened gloved fists, took a deep breath, and stood. He quickly wiped a fist across each eye and turned to me. "Yes, Master Thomas, of course we do. She was our daughter. We had not wanted to make it well-known. Bad enough she died, bad enough there had to be an investigation. But when it yielded no answers, we had to make our facts firm."

"Why?"

Lord Pendrel sighed and shook his head. "I suppose it's another one of those things no one talks about, being a lord. To not know, even after all resources have been spent searching for facts. That kind of ineptitude simply isn't acceptable. And how could no one know? How could *no one* see what happened?" His eyes were sharp on me, and there was a pleading tone in his voice.

"Was she on her own a lot?" I asked.

He continued to stare at me, his face turning by degrees to sadness, then anguish. "I don't know," he whispered. He set his jaw, struggled to master himself. "She was not often with *me*. She had the Lady Pendrel, and her nurse, Penelope, to look after her."

"Where were they all?"

"The Lady Pendrel was not well, and had given her to Penelope. Penelope had to...excuse herself, a moment, and told my daughter to wait outside. When she came out, Joliette was gone." His face spasmed again and he cleared his throat. He tugged on his gauntlets. "She was gone. Penelope was not worried at first—as you say, she was sometimes alone. But after a time Penelope became frantic. She found the Fool, who assured her Joliette had gone back to her mother."

"Did any of them see her with her Ladyship?"

Lord Pendrel turned to gaze at the castle. I could almost sense him looking through the walls to the ground below the tower, and I knew his answer: the next time anyone had seen her was after she had fallen. "Lordship, was the dragon already showing himself by then? Or was it after?"

"What did the archives tell you?" he asked distantly.

"It is difficult to say, Lordship. There are references almost as far back as we can go. But never that it was visible until more recently.

But if it caused her to fall..."

"It had not interacted physically—still has not, to my knowledge."

"But if it frightened her..."

He turned to me. "What difference would it make?"

I shook my head. "I don't know if it will or not, Lordship. Maybe Rae-Anna will have an idea. But we have to know the truth, either way, to figure anything out."

He blew out a breath, and it turned to frost in front of him. He glanced toward the mountains. "It is drawing late," he said. "Cold will descend quickly. Let us ride back, and I will think."

"Lordship..."

He cocked an eyebrow at me.

I sighed. "Sir, forgive me. I don't know my station, certainly don't see myself more than a farmer, to question such a man as yourself..."

"Ask it, and if needs be I will warn you only."

I gazed into his eyes, tried to meet him as a man. "You have impressed me with your preparedness, the ways you manage your demesne. I may not understand left from right in it, but it appears to me to be good. But to not remember when a dragon began appearing—" I cut myself off just as his hand began to wave. "Forgive me, Lordship," I said, bowing my head.

I startled as his hand came to rest gently on my shoulder. I looked up.

"No, you do well to ask. It helps not that I have wrestled with that same question to fruitless end. I pray, Master Thomas—and mere farmer, you are not—that your wintering here does not have the same effect concerning the dragon with you, as it seems to with everyone else here."

"No one remembers when it first showed up?" I asked.

He shook his head solemnly. "As I said, we have investigated most thoroughly."

"Of course, yes, Lordship," I said.

He gave a squeeze on my shoulder, and we mounted. When I looked to Mahmoud, he only stared back at me and I couldn't help but wonder why Rae-Anna thought he should come with us. And I thought, by his expression, that he wondered the same thing.

"My lord," I said as we cantered toward the gate. "Why do you think Rae-Anna and I will have any more luck figuring out the mystery of the dragon than yourself?"

"Are you sure I do?" he asked. He grinned at me. "You were the ones telling me you came here for it. Am I wrong to take you at your word?"

"I hope not, Lordship."

His grin faded, but only a little. "So do I," he said. "And the hope I have, Thomas, is that this dragon is borne of the spirit realm—and I am not one equipped to handle it."

"You have no priests or anyone here, lordship?"

We reached the gate, and he paused to swing his gaze across his lands one last time. "They left. Last winter. Apparently they were not equipped to handle it either."

I let them precede me, unsettled a little by his statement. Mahmoud, finally, drew up beside me and stopped. "You are well?" he asked.

I shook my head. "Oh, fine I suppose. I wonder sometimes what Rae-Anna has gotten us into."

"With this...dragon?"

I glanced quickly at him as we both nudged our mounts forward through the gate. "No, pretty much since Holden."

He glanced sharply at me. "You do not doubt her?"

"It's not so much her, I guess. Just, whatever it is we're supposed to be doing."

"Ah. You doubt your god."

"I...hmm. I guess not. But I run out of choices, don't I?"

He cocked an eyebrow. "If you trust your god, and trust your woman..."

"Right. But it seems a little strange, doesn't it? Sometimes it doesn't feel real—or like we can do anything. I mean, who are we compared to whatever clergy was here, and left?"

"You do not know them. And you did more than your...clergy? In Holden."

"Yeah. Well, she did most of that. I came a little late."

"And I was not part of it at all."

I sighed. "What do you think of the dragon, and the child?"

He shrugged. "I do not see them."

I reined in the horse and turned to him. "You don't?" He shook his head. "But you don't question it?"

He studied me. "I trust your woman," he said.

"But not our god?"

His eyes glittered. "I do not know him."

"Didn't he heal your mortal wound?"

"Your woman—Rae-Anna—did that."

I spared him a glance as we continued forward. Lord Pendrel and his entourage were getting further ahead. "Mahmoud, I've known Rae-Anna for many years and I can promise you she cannot heal things like that." We continued in silence for a few streets before a thought wandered into my mind. "She mentioned that you acted like—not that you knew her, but were expecting her. Something like that?"

We reached the stables, and he stopped a way back from them as Lord Pendrel dismounted ahead of us. "Not expected," he said.

"Warned."

"Warned against Rae-Anna?" I asked, incredulous. "What about her?"

"Do you know Azrael?" I shook my head. "Azrael is also the Angel of Death. He is...a messenger. A guide. To take me to my final resting place after death."

"Okay." I didn't feel like arguing religion just then, so I listened.

"When I departed, a seer told me that one would snatch me from Azrael, but only for a short time. That this one would bring me another death—would carry an *akil allahm*."

"What's that?"

"Flesh devourer."

My eyebrows went up. "Oh."

He examined me. "Do you believe me?"

I scoffed. Lightly. "Mahmoud, since Rae-Anna told me about her fire, I've had to believe a lot stranger things than that. The question I have is, do you believe her?"

"I believe the seer. Rae-Anna did take me from Azrael. I heard his steps as I lay at the convent."

"I remember. Well, not hearing steps, but seeing you. So what does a flesh devourer do?"

"Devours flesh."

I deserved that. "How does it do that, though?"

"The seer did not say."

Lord Pendrel's horses were stabled, and he and his entourage had departed. Our meeting was at an end, apparently. The hostler looked at Mahmoud and I expectantly, so I took the time to think as we helped unlade them and put them in their stalls.

"This seer," I said finally as we made our way back to the keep, "was he Muslim as well?"

"Of course."

I considered the Seed, the tangle of branches growing from it, sorting through the leaves as they spread. I wondered if Rae-Anna's Fire required as much thought to parse through what it said, or if it came more as impressions. Something to ask her later. "I only ask because, in Our Father's kingdom, the flesh is not just what we see, but part of our nature that makes us who we are. Especially the corrupted part—the part always trying to make us evil."

"You already think I am evil," he said bluntly.

I took a breath, parted another set of branches. "I guess...don't take it personally? Well, and we're all evil—or, we still have evil parts of us. I still do. Rae-Anna still does. But only through the power of The Beloved do we hope to overcome it."

He shook his head. "I do not know which I think more foolish," he muttered.

"Anyway, if we believe the spirit realm is all one, then perhaps your seer saw into something that Our Father was trying to show you, even if the seer didn't acknowledge Our Father the way we do."

"Allah and Your Father are one," he said.

I was getting into territory I didn't know. "Well, okay. I thought they were not. But let's say they are. Our Holy Word says that we are to crucify the flesh, essentially destroy it, in order to better and more easily obey Our Father. So perhaps what your seer saw in Rae-Anna was that she would bring something that would help you destroy your sinful nature."

"Your Beloved?"

I nodded. "And the Sacred Fire." Why was it called that, when mine was a Seed? I wondered if Rae-Anna would know, if she even realized. I worried that maybe I did have something different—either corrupted, or replaced—from Mr. Messick? I hadn't relied on it much during our journey south from Holden. I was too worried back then about learning swordplay from Mahmoud. Had *he* somehow done something? I watched him to see if his expression betrayed anything. But he didn't have an expression. Either way, when I first started really paying attention to it after the first time, it was always a Seed.

"You think too much of your Beloved," he said, and shook his head. "A great prophet, surely. But he cannot have this great power you give him. He is not Allah, and says so."

I opened my mouth to reply, then squinted. "Does he?"

"'*The Lord our God is one Lord.*' Yet you suddenly say he is three."

"Oh, quoting the Elder Holy Words?" I asked. Mahmoud nodded. "Okay, he does say that—quotes that. But then he also says elsewhere: *And now, O Father, glorify thou me with thine own self with the glory which I had with thee before the world was.*' There are other places as well where he definitely equates himself with Our Father, existed with him from the beginning."

Mahmoud was silent as we passed through into the inner courts. As we neared where he would go off to his own room he paused. "Thank you, Thomas, for your respectful discussion," he said. He bowed and departed before I could reply, hands clasped behind his back.

I heard footsteps and turned. Sister Judith's bony hand grasped my wrist. "About time, boy," she rasped. Her voice grated, her skin pulled so tight against her face I could see her skull. Fires raged in her eyes—anger, and lust. "I've had enough waiting for you to reject that demon-spawn, that trollop! Come to me, come to my bower. Come!"

I gasped shallow breaths, waited for the vision to pass. Surely it was only Rae-Anna who surprised me, The Liar who twisted her features. And her words?

As though hearing my thoughts, Judith cackled. "Twisted or un-twisted, you both will join me. Sacred Fire indeed! Death's con-flagration, rather! Even now it desiccates your seed. It hardens, shrivels, cracks, blackens, pops! Come to me instead, come taste of me, plunge deep into my healing waters. Only I have been blessed by The Beloved!" At the name her mouth opened wide, a roaring furnace that rose to a shriek. It seemed to consume her insides, and she crumpled as she deflated. I fell, finally, scrabbling backward as the figure of Rae-Anna resolved itself from Judith's fading ghost. The horror on her face magnified my own.

"Thomas, what is it?" she cried. Tears coursed down her cheeks—her marred, beautiful cheeks, running in irregular rivulets across her scars.

I gasped one final time, feeling my own eyes burn. "She's not gone yet," I whispered. I buried my face in my hands. "She's not gone."

I heard Rae-Anna's soft footfalls approach, her cloak rustle. I looked up as she knelt in front of me, just outside arms' reach. "Who isn't gone, Thomas?"

I focused on her eyes. I saw her inner fire burning in them—gently, warmly, the fire of a hearth at the end of a cold day. It seeped into me. Judith's study never had a fire. She never seemed to need heat, no matter the season. I took a deep breath, let Rae-Anna's fire leech in and tend my seed, light the shriveled leaves. Steady waters flowed around it, and it drank. Life returned to the leaves and branches, but it retreated back into the soil. Healed, but buried. Maybe it needed more time to truly regenerate. Darkness covered the soil. I turned away from it.

"Who else is there?" I said. I leaned back, finding the wall near me.

Rae-Anna sighed. She sounded broken too. "Judith," she offered. I didn't even have to nod. There was silence, broken only by our breathing, until Rae-Anna spoke first. "Why did they keep her there? 'A bruised reed shall he not break,' and yet it was her special purview to break as many bruised reeds as she could, as though personally insulted or injured by them."

I snorted. That definitely seemed like her job. "It's not just her fault, though," I muttered.

"You said you didn't want her advances," Rae-Anna said hesitantly.

I stared at her. "You doubt me again?"

Her eyes fell and she reached out tenderly, but shied away from touching my leg. I sighed hard. "What a vision of a man I am," I spat. "I've seen stray cats with more courage."

"I'm sorry, Thomas," she said, her voice strained with exhaustion and frustration.

I felt the ground over the seed harden, ever so slightly. Enough to recognize, and enough of a farmer remained in me to know I couldn't let that lie. "No, I'm sorry," I said. "Please, come sit with me. Here." I patted the floor next to me. She came and sat, and I pulled her close. I still had to grit my teeth, remind myself three times that doing so did not put me on a level with Judith. When I leaned over to kiss her hair I smelled her—Rae-Anna, no other. No, this was blessed by The Beloved. I was not Judith who took advantage of innocence, and Rae-Anna was almost an entirely different creature from that woman. I held Rae-Anna tighter, held my beloved tighter, allowed her fire to shine in me again.

"I said it wasn't entirely her fault, because I was the one who chased you into the convent," I said. "I could have stayed away, let you pursue the life you wanted—"

"I didn't necessarily want that, Thomas, I felt I had no choice."

I kissed her again. "Right. I'm sorry. But neither of us knew that at the time. I feel like if I hadn't been pursuing you, I wouldn't have come across Judith. If Our Father intended us to be together, He would have found a way without me chasing it. By trying to speed up His timing, I opened myself to...what happened."

She twisted to look at me. "Why did you pursue me?" she asked.

Oh, help me. "Can I *not* tell you that?"

Her lips twisted into a grin. "Why can't you tell me?"

"Does it matter? I did, and here we are, and everything worked out. Mostly."

"Thomas..."

"Fine. But don't look at me. I'm serious!" She shook her head, but looked away. "Okay, so, remember when I ran into you outside the inn? You were looking at one of the horses some merchant had ridden in on, and we were talking about horses in general, but you mentioned how this one didn't seem well-kept after—I said don't look at me!"

She huffed. "Well, get on with it at least."

"Okay. Well, we went inside the barn together, and you leaned over one of the stalls to get a brush or something. And...that."

She turned and stared at me. "'That'...what?"

"Well. You know..."

"That I cared for a horse?"

I rolled my eyes. "No, though that's nice too. No, the actual...reaching into the stall..."

She continued to stare at me, until suddenly her cheeks flamed red and she hit me in the shoulder. "Thomas!"

"You asked!"

"Oh Beloved help us." She put a hand over her face as she shook her head. But she was still smiling. "Really? Through three layers of dress—"

"Didn't matter."

"Clearly." She hit me again, softer this time, then leaned her head against me. "Well, as you said, I guess it worked out. So far."

"You're not disgusted with me?"

"I guess not. It is kind of nice to know, in a way." She picked at a thread of her dress. "But also makes it a little harder..."

"I know," I said quickly. I didn't want to talk about it again. But I didn't push her away. That counted for something, right?

Joliff found us still like that, but merely raised a brow. "Dinner time," he said simply, then turned slightly away to wait for us. As we climbed to our feet, a thought struck me.

"Rae-Anna, who did you think I meant when I said she wasn't gone?"

She paused in brushing off her dress. "Oh, that. It was strange, because I had just heard those exact words not long before. When the dragon showed up earlier than usual."

"By who?"

"Lady Pendrel."

Chapter 7

I tried to focus on the dinner. I was mostly successful. And it was made easier by the amount I knew I would blush when I thought of Thomas' admission, and did not want the questions. But like a minstrel, whenever it grew quiet, there it was filling in the space. It had helped, at least in those moments of wondering if Thomas was even attracted to me. Obviously, he was. Or had been. I did manage not to dwell on questions of my disfigurement.

But it also made the relationship—the beginnings of it—much shallower. And, in my honest moments, I knew much of my attraction to him in the early days had been on his eyes, and his muscled arms. At least, I thought perhaps if I was held in those arms I would be safe from the judgements of others. It had certainly not been based on the soundness of his character. But that had come with time. And if it had not come, I would have turned him away.

Would he do the same for me?

As I watched him, listened to the conversations he managed to keep with their Lord and Ladyship, I knew he would. No man would go through what he was going through for a pretty...whatever about me was still pretty in his eyes. And, as Aurden proved, beauty was fleeting. For the cloud of uncertainties surrounding our relationship, and our mission for The Beloved, Thomas' faithfulness to me I could not question.

He would not leave me. But as he continued to struggle with his torments brought by Sister Judith, I hoped I would maintain enough faith to let him stay. Not because I needed some special fulfillment, as I had found men did—even cursed with left-handedness, I was not bereft of those types of men while a stray in Holden—but simply because the relationship felt so lacking.

At least, that's what I thought at the time. Part of it, I believe, was because of the number of lascivious men I had encountered. I wondered what it would be like to be the object of a pure desire instead. Another part, I'm sure, was the expectation that I should carry a child. Many, actually. And so as I looked at Lady Pendrel, I wondered why she had only the one. She hadn't told me. Of her many regrets, she had not mentioned anything surrounding her fertility.

After Thomas had left that morning with Lord Pendrel, I stood atop one of the ramparts, wrapped in a thick fur cape I had found in our bedchamber shortly after we arrived. His Lordship was correct: the sun was not as chill as it could get in wintertime. But the wind off the mountains, especially high up on the ramparts, was unkind. And so I stood, wrapped in fur I could never hope to own, watching my husband ride off with his Lordship and a bevy of retainers. And I had just the briefest thought that Thomas and Lord Pendrel might switch places—or, at least, Thomas might step into that role, and I his Lady.

A cloud passed briefly and I turned from the vision, and from the scene below me. "My Lady!" I exclaimed, surprised to see her hesitating at the doorway. Her hands fidgeted.

"That had once been mine, did you know?" she asked, nodding toward my fur cape.

"I had not meant to assume, milady," I said hurriedly, making to take it off.

She laughed, suddenly—or decidedly—at ease, and I knew it was okay. She watched me with sparkling eyes as she neared the wall. "It fits you well," she said. "Perhaps, if you survive your time with us, I will let you keep it."

I nodded my thanks and wrapped it tight again. "Do you think, my Lady, there is a chance we will not survive?"

She was silent for a time, looking out over the valley southward. Thomas and the others were drawing a wide circle. "Survival is...can be a difficult standard," Lady Pendrel murmured. She glanced at me. "I forget—you likely understand what I mean."

I cocked my head, glanced away. "Nothing is promised, Lady, except surviving—until the time we are called home. There are days—have been days for us already—where we have survived abundantly."

We both chuckled, but she sobered first. "And others where you have survived only scantly. Do you think—do you ever feel that surviving is not enough? That to be called home would be the best for everyone?"

I opened my mouth, but waited a moment. Just enough to feel the Fire inside. *"For I am in a strait betwixt two, having a desire to depart, and to be with The Beloved; which is far better: nevertheless to abide in the flesh is more needful for you."*

She gave me a dim smile. "It must be nice to be needed."

"I did not say I felt needed, my Lady. I merely said what the Sacred

Fire told me to say."

"I have seen the way your Thomas looks at you: he needs you as seeds need water."

I smiled, recalling Thomas' parting words. They needed heat too, apparently. Lady Pendrel did not need to know that part, though. "And I have seen the way your people look to you, Lady," I chided.

She snorted softly. "Ah, yes, the people. Without whom I might find peace and comfort on a farm somewhere."

I stared at her. "Surely...you did not come from a farm..."

She arched an eyebrow. "Why say you? Because my hands are not still calloused? Because there is no soil on my dress?"

"I-I'm sorry Lady, I meant no offense. I simply didn't think it worked that way—"

She snorted again, gentler this time, as she smiled. "No, it does not. But shall we say I married up. Lord Pendrel was as far above my station as any other lord would be to a peasant, and it caused nearly as much scandal. At least for the first several years."

"What happened? What changed, I mean?"

"Apparently I did very well," Lady Pendrel said with a mock curtsy. "I behaved myself at court; I attended the correct parties, wearing the correct attire; sent the appropriate gifts; and hid my true feelings flawlessly—just as any high-born lady should."

"Why do you stop now?"

Her face lit up as she squinted at me. "Do you think I'm wicked? Or just a hypocrite?"

I shrugged. "Our Beloved perhaps did not distinguish between the two, Lady," I said frankly. "But I sense neither in you. We all bear responsibilities—some far more than others," I added, inclining my head toward her. "But we all wish to be rid of them at least once in a while. And if we are with the correct person."

She nodded back to me. "I have been unfair. You didn't know this is where I come to escape just those responsibilities, and now I have taken out my anger on you."

"I appreciate your candor, Lady." I cocked my head. "Is that why Mistress Pendrel came out here as well?"

Her face went stiff as she looked away. "Do you think I was a bad mother?" she asked. "Overbearing? That I drove her to—"

"Ladyship, even The Beloved left his parents, and for three days they could not find him. Those were perhaps different circumstances but... All children feel the burden of responsibility, and wish to escape."

Lady Pendrel hugged herself under her cloak. "Perhaps. I don't know why she came up here. Sometimes I didn't even know she did it." She eyed me. "Do not think I was inattentive. It was precisely because I didn't want her constantly watched, hovered over. Every moment of her day and night dictated to her."

"As yours was?"

Her eyes widened, but she quickly set her jaw. "It was my fault," she said. "I was—I fought against it harder than I should have. Perhaps if I had been a little more...malleable. My parents were not harsh people, not at first. Isabelle got it far worse than me, in the end."

"Isabelle?"

"My older sister. When the list of rules began to grow, she grew into them—as she was supposed to. One needs not the rod if the child is already unspoilt," she said as though quoting. I wondered if it were a family proverb. "Isabelle proved that. As I began to grow into the rules she had already followed for years, I rebelled. I wonder, sometimes..." She trailed off, then shook herself. "Useless, wondering."

"When did you meet his Lordship?"

She grinned again. "That was also my fault. Tell me, Rae-Anna, was Thomas your first choice?"

I took a breath, wondering where she was going and thinking I needed to head her off. "There was a time when Sisterhood was my first choice," I said carefully. "Our relationship did not begin easily..." I too trailed off, realizing the relationship was not continuing that easily either.

"But was there someone your parents wanted for you instead?"

I snorted. "My parents wished only that I would not be demon-possessed," I said. "But I think you are not asking out of curiosity."

"I'll leave it alone," she said. "I wanted you to pity me, I suppose. My parents had a man chosen for me—well within my station, from a nearby demesne, less remote, less...austere." She shivered in the wind, glanced around the valley surrounding the castle, and chuckled again. "They told me to mind myself when Lord Pendrel—that was Lord Pendrel's father, then—came through. I was to remain in my chambers with my nurse until he and his entourage had gone. Another rule I needed to break." She shook her head. "Despite my nurse's stringent protests I dressed myself—not provocatively, but neither was I demure—and made sure I was seen wandering the halls." She laughed. "My father went nearly apoplectic. But of course that was not seemly." Her laughter and smile faded to a point she nearly frowned. "A month later the letter came, requiring my family, and especially I, attend the Lordship and his son for a banquet. We were wed the following summer."

"You said Isabelle got it worse?" I asked quietly.

Lady Pendrel shook her head and I saw a tear drip down her cheek. "She actually loved the man to whom she was betrothed. But he was not as important as the man I was supposed to wed. So when I went with Lord Pendrel, she had to marry the one I had been promised to. And he was...displeased." She swiped her hand against her cheek. "She has not been seen publicly in ten years, and her last letter to me hinted at some of how he treated her. None of my letters back to her have had a response. I don't think she gets them anymore. All because I had to show myself off."

I did not like how close her story was to mine. I pushed it aside as best I could. "It is possible, Lady, that he would have treated *you* the same for some other perceived slight."

"Do you think that makes it better?"

"No, Ladyship. I only mean that life is often bitter for one reason or another—and can hurt those we love more than ourselves despite all of our sacrifices. Or obedience."

"Or disobedience?"

I grimaced, and looked off down the valley. Thomas and his Lordship were already heading back. I wondered if his conversation was going any better. Surely—but just then they turned and rode toward the mountains. This view, I had to admit, was spectacular. No corner of the lands could hide from this vantage point. "When we disobey Our Father, it is very easy to stray into things that harm us—things He would have kept us from had we obeyed." I looked at her, fixed her with my gaze and let her see my scars. "But sometimes, too, obedience will take us into the heart of danger. And we do not always come out unscathed."

"You don't regret it?" she asked.

I blinked. "What part?"

She waved her hand. "Any of it. Leaving your home, leaving the Sisters, being with Thomas, staying in Aurden and dealing with...whatever it was you dealt with...coming here..."

"There are many things I wish could have happened differently," I said. "I would have saved others from a great deal of pain if I could have—"

"Others? Not yourself?"

I clenched my jaw, tried not to look out again and find Thomas riding far below. "I suppose...the pain of others often comes to us as well, Ladyship. I don't deny you that. But regretting it..." I wanted to say I couldn't understand it, but I knew that would be false. I couldn't understand regretting things for myself, I suppose. "I do not see what I would have done differently. Perhaps knowing what I do now—but we cannot do that, can we?"

"I knew enough back then," she replied. "I knew enough, but chose against it. How much has changed because of it? I would still have had a daughter, I would think. Still would have served my Lord and the people of his demesne. Still might have been the perfect Lady at court and all the rest."

"What did change, then?"

She glanced across at where the dragon's tower had appeared before, where was only empty air now. "I might still have a daughter."

"What can you tell me about that day?" I asked.

She shook her head. "I've gone over it a thousand times. A thousand moments that might have changed the outcome. If I had done this, not done that, said this, insisted upon..." She paused, shook her head again. "The investigation was thorough. And exhausting, quite frankly. I still don't know if I grieved, do you know that?" She stared hard at me. "Martin returned so quickly, began questioning everyone—including me. Tirelessly, almost. Except how much he tired the rest of us with it."

"Perhaps that was his way of grieving," I offered.

"Hmm. Of course. So he got to grieve, but I did not."

"What would you do? If you were able?"

Her mouth opened and closed a few times as she glanced sightlessly around the valley. "Fine. I don't know. I don't know how to grieve a daughter who—" She sucked down a sob. Her hand went to her mouth to still the trembling. Slowly it curled into a fist. "I'm not allowed!" Her eyes glistened. "Grief doesn't go to court, to parties. It is not proper attire. I feigned the grief I thought people wanted to see, to be proper and well accoutered. So people could stand in corners and nod sagely saying 'the Lady Pendrel grieves a daughter' for just long enough to be appropriate. And then we moved on." She glared at me as tears coursed down her face. "We moved on! Our lives move on ceaselessly, reeling from one event to another, one day, one week, one year to another with no proper reflection or meditation on what on earth is happening to us!" She dashed angrily at her tears. "And now what am I supposed to do? I can't go back and grieve her—what would people think? I was supposed to have been done. Now I'll look the madwoman. And so here I am, stuck in this ridiculous castle with its ridiculous dragon and my ridiculous life, all paint and plaster, with no power to slow it down or even change its course. How can I not think about how I should have just stayed in my room with my nurse and done some cursed needlework?"

I was at a loss. I gaped a few moments before remembering to sink into the Sacred Fire. *Rejoice with them that do rejoice, and weep with them that weep.* I hoped it would not be inappropriate as I stepped toward her and hugged her. She fell into my embrace, and though she did not weep openly I could tell she cried.

We stayed thus for a time, until I felt her stiffen and I stepped quickly away. When I looked at her face again, I could tell the Lady was back. I turned to the wall, back to enjoying the view. She stepped up beside me. "Was the castle just like this when you first arrived?"

I asked. "I was somewhat struck by awe when we first topped the ridge."

"Oh yes," she said. "Except I came at the end of summer—we were wed at my father's demesne, further west. But the fields were ripe, the land fair bursting with grains and animals and fruits. I remember it was difficult making the descent for the number of merchants and farmers clogging the road. I was terrified we'd be caught in a storm, or something. They were supposed to happen frequently in the mountains. But I knew I should not lack as Lady of the manor."

"Thomas and I have been trying to figure out when the dragon first appeared. It seems to have existed in the lore surrounding it, but no one had actually seen it until more recently."

She glanced aside again, I could tell without looking that she sought the dragon's tower. "It does blur together," she murmured. Her eyes focused on me. "As you say, it was much a part of the castle's lore—so much you could imagine it when the stories were told around a winter night's fire. And of course when it appeared, it looked exactly as you would expect it. So it just seemed like you had to have seen it before." She chewed her lip, caught herself, and smiled with chagrin. "You're bringing the 'old me' back, you know," she said.

Suddenly she went deathly white, her eyes goggling. I followed her gaze, and there was the tower, the dragon soaring on the wind. His scales glittered in the sun, though an indigo darkness oozed from him like smoke from a smoldering brush-pile. A strange terror struck me, not of physical pain, but as though the worst parts of my past were about to be laid bare. I had a strange urge to cover Lady Pendrel's ears—to cover my own—to keep the noise of his voice away from both of us.

He arced lazily. But when he spied us on the tower, I could see in his eyes the intent of a hunter. His wings snapped wide, his body like a lance to the knight's helm. But he did not aim for me. I looked back at Lady Pendrel, saw his form reflected small in her eyes. When he breathed fire, it came not as a hearth magnified but rather as a cloud of words, all tumbled together and on top of each other. I heard mutterings, gossips, judgements, secrets, grief, and blame billowing and consuming.

I don't know why, but I reeled into her, knocked her over and onto the top of the tower. The storm of words rolled over us, still muttering, but I could somehow tell it had not got her. As the dragon showed us his back, I looked up and saw the little girl—Mistress Pendrel—standing near the ramparts and also watching the dragon.

"She's not gone yet!" Lady Pendrel cried. "She's still here! Joliette!" She rose, arms outstretched as she ran to her daughter.

"Lady, no!" I cried after her. Again I threw myself at her, managed to grab hold of her cloak just as she was about to go over the wall. Joliette had disappeared and I heard a faint scream on the wind, falling away. The servants appeared, grasping Lady Pendrel and pulling her away from the edge. As they hustled her away and down the stairs, I suddenly saw Lord Pendrel and Thomas come out of the woods far away. Numbly I followed Lady Pendrel, hoping Thomas would soon return inside.

Thomas' hand came to rest on my arm, pulling me from my reverie. The meal was finishing, so I hurriedly ate what was left in front of me, smiling at the servant as she took my platter—one of the few left. I had missed almost the entirety of the conversation, so I let half an ear listen while I sank back into the Fire.

And when the servant of the man of God was risen early, and gone forth, behold, an host compassed the city both with horses and chariots.

Chapter 8

Needless to say, I did not sleep well that night.

A castle makes all sorts of noises in the dead of night. Winds leaking through the corridors can rustle tapestries and sound very much like someone knocking on a faraway door. Mice who have found a haven from the cold scurry along the stone, claws ticking and clicking like very large spiders—or rats. Thomas would suddenly roll over, and I thought he had heard something as well and was preparing for battle. Perhaps someone would be up using the garderobe, and I would try to listen so intently only to have the air turn to wool, and my own blood pulse in my ears so that my mind filled in noises where there were none.

Eventually my breathing relaxed. The castle—after an almost frenetic night-time routine—seemed to settle in as though its breathing relaxed too. I rested in the Fire, leaned into Thomas' back, and almost dozed.

At first I thought it was another breeze stealing through some chink in the walls, some other tapestry far down the hall rattling. But the sound grew louder, distinct, measured. A heavy clinking, nearly echoing but each reverberation bitten off. Rhythmic, but I could count almost a whole breath between strikes. And it grew louder.

Louder, or closer.

It rang like a chain, each link dropped into some vessel. I could almost feel the weight of it pressing down, building and growing. My breaths came harder and my limbs heavier. I wanted to wake Thomas but could not. I could not cry out, could not even roll my head over with enough force to butt his shoulder.

I strained my eyes to see, but the darkness was complete. We had drawn the curtains too tight at the window. Then, as the chains continued to rattle, I thought I heard voices behind it, a great multitude. At first there were too many voices, the words indistinguishable. But they all moaned a lament—that I could tell. Like a great wind through the trees their cries rose and fell inharmoniously, but all unanimously weeping. The chains continued to ring.

Clink!

Clink!

Clink!

In between the moans, when they together would die away for a moment, I heard frantic whispers, monotone, like a susurrus of a hundred adders slithering through dried leaves. These, too, I could not distinguish. But there was no urgency to the voices, just an intense repetition as though they were desperate to remind themselves of some horror, either lived through or feared. It became a dreadful choir of moans and manic whispers with the terrible chains keeping time.

Suddenly, one whisper stood out among the rest, and it called out in between the pounding of the iron.

Clink!

"You."

Clink!

"Stand."

Clink!

"CONDEMNED!"

Two great orbs like coals glowed in the darkness, lighting in an instant the terrible face and dripping fangs of the dragon as he reared above us. His saliva struck like acid, hissing and smoking. My mouth gaped for a moment but my throat was squeezed tight. His final word became a roar that first covered my scream, so I only became aware I was shrieking as my throat began to burn and my lungs emptied.

Thomas was up, feet rooted in the stone, his arms spread wide as branches, and I could swear he swelled in stature—an oak after a hundred seasons of rain and sun and tilled earth—nearly blotting from my vision the dragon on the other side of him. The coals exploded in brilliance, momentarily blinding me and chasing every shadow from the room. When I could see again, Thomas wielded a sword brilliant as forge-fresh steel. The dragon's roar abated, almost seemed concerned at what stood against him.

Thomas' voice thundered down upon that dragon with the weight of mountains as he cried: *"Thou comest to me with a sword, and with a spear, and with a shield: but I come to thee in the name of The Beloved of hosts, Our Father of the armies of Israel, whom thou hast defied."*

With a great whirling sound the lights that now I could only see against the walls dimmed, the chains rattled as though drawn swiftly away, and all those who moaned and whispered snapped their mouths shut as darkness filled the room once more.

Tremors wracked my body as I shivered. I sensed more than saw Thomas turn and come back to me. I almost thought to feel rough bark and cool leaves brushing across me. But as he pulled me into his arms all I felt were farmer's hands and corded muscles, and I sank into him as into a cooling stream on a sweltering summer day.

I wept uncontrollably. And, somehow, at some point, I fell asleep.

I awoke gradually, slowly. Birds were twittering outside our window, and I felt the rise and fall of Thomas' chest under my head. A hair pulled at the corner of my lip and I tugged it free, working my tongue around to wet my mouth. I took a deep breath, and sighed.

"We need to figure out how to get rid of that dragon," Thomas said.

"Mmhmm."

"Are you okay?"

I snuggled my head tighter into his shirt, gripped him a little tighter around his waist. "Yes."

He stroked my hair. "What happened? I only woke up for the end."

"That was probably the most important part," I murmured. I began to describe to him what led up to his waking, as he continued to stroke my hair, combing it occasionally with his fingers. "Then you woke up, and stood between me and it like a strong oak tree. I couldn't even see him anymore, just the light on the walls from his eyes."

"But you can't remember what the voices were saying?"

I shook my head, then propped myself up suddenly on my elbow as I recognized his tone—as though he knew, and thought I should too. "Wait, did you hear them?"

He was frowning, with a faraway look in his eyes, though his gaze was on my face. He sucked a breath in through his nose. "Yeah."

I continued to stare at him, waiting for him to continue.

"There was a lot, so I couldn't catch all of it. But the ones who moaned had died, were crying from beyond the grave for all the decisions that had gotten them there. One of them..." He closed his eyes, and a tear leaked out from one corner. I reached up and placed my hand on his cheek. He pressed into it a moment, then took a breath. "One of them was Joliette," he said, his eyes focused on mine, now.

"Did she say anything?"

He shook his head. "Their words weren't distinct. I don't know how I know what they were crying about, but I could sense it. There weren't actual words, just the emotions."

"Were they—were they in Abaddon?"

He frowned. "I don't...I mean, a child shouldn't be, right? How could they...how could Our Father—"

"No, I think you're right," I said quickly. "Not a child. You're sure it was her?"

"I never met her," he said with a brief, wry grin. "But I knew that it was supposed to be her."

"Hmm," I murmured, suddenly skeptical. "What about the voices you could distinguish?"

"Well, like I said, there were a lot of them, and they didn't exactly let each other talk. They were—"

"I noticed they seemed very intent on saying what they needed to."

He nodded. "Oh, very. None of it was directed at us, though," he said, somehow answering a question I hadn't asked yet. "Not to say it won't be important... Anyway, this is apparently a very dangerous castle."

I couldn't keep a grin from creeping onto my face. "Oh, is it really?"

He rubbed my back. "Yeah." But he sobered quickly. "More dangerous than that, though. Most of the people here, don't belong here."

Now my brow furrowed. "What do you mean? Like, they aren't

serfs here?"

"Oh, they are now. Sort of. They came as travelers, like we did. But now they can't leave."

"Um..."

"Exactly. It was hard to pick out. Some sounded like they owed Lord Pendrel something they were working off, but felt they would never be able to. Some sounded like he didn't care if they came or went, but they just never found themselves back on their way. Some—" He swallowed hard. "Some had messages for their families, to come save them or..." His voice died to a whisper. "Or warning them to stay far, far away."

I laid my head back down as I tried to think. Were we stuck, without realizing? I didn't know how to find out without trying to leave, but it was the Sacred Fire that I felt kept us here. Would Lord Pendrel feel we owed him for all the feasts? "Should we stay for morning meal?" I wondered aloud. "Maybe that's what keeps them here."

"No. I mean, I don't think that matters. And Mahmoud has come and gone—they know him well, here."

"True. Maybe they don't want him. Lord Pendrel didn't seem particularly fond of him."

"We'll have to ask him later. Mahmoud, that is. But there was more. One voice in particular, that almost sounded like it belonged with the others—the first, the ones moaning and crying from...wherever they were doing that from. But it wasn't with them." He shook his head. "It was strange—even his, or its, voice wasn't always clear. But from what I could tell, he had murdered Joliette."

My head snapped up. "She *was* murdered?"

He nodded slowly. "It sounded like it. It's hard. So much of it was a sense of knowing, being able to feel what was behind the words, more than just the words themselves."

"Who was it?"

He shook his head. "I don't know. No idea."

"But...I mean, who were they? You said he sounded like he belonged with the others, but where were *they*? Where was he? What was—?"

He grinned, lightly pressing a finger to my lips. "One at a time. The others were beyond the grave. The whisperers were still alive."

"The murderer is still alive."

"Ah. Yes."

"And you've no idea who it is."

"Nope."

I stared. A little annoyed, honestly. "Thomas, there are hundreds of people here. And Lord Pendrel already talked to everyone, at least so Lady Pendrel said."

"Yes, he said that too."

I chewed the corner of my lip. "Why couldn't I hear them? What they were actually saying?"

He shrugged. "Maybe because you were awake?"

"How do you know I was awake?"

"Weren't you?"

I set my jaw and stared at him.

He started rubbing my back again. "I don't know how I know this," he said. "But everyone we could hear was awake. And...I could hear you, too."

My eyes went wide as I tried to remember what I had been thinking about. "What did I say?"

He swallowed. "I tried not to pay too much attention."

"Oh, so I was talking to you but you wanted to ignore me?" I was half-joking when I asked. But I did wonder.

"Rae-Anna, they were deeply personal thoughts I was hearing, most of them. I didn't want to hear something in a dream or something that you wouldn't want to tell me on your own..."

"Oh," I said. That actually made sense. "I—Thank you."

"But..."

I gazed at him, willing him to continue, but also afraid. "What is it, Thomas?" I pleaded as the silence dragged on.

"I know what the Holy Words say about marriage and all. But I don't... I mean, we didn't really know—you didn't know how badly off I was because of..." He wagged his head. *"Her.* So if you want—if you needed to change your mind..."

"Thomas!" I cried. I buried my face in his chest, held him as tightly as I could and hoped he wasn't put off by it. "I never thought that, ever," I pleaded into his shirt. Pleaded, because though I had never thought it directly, I couldn't deny that some of my thoughts would have eventually led there. I looked up at him. "Knowing or not doesn't matter to me, I knew enough. And you have already given me so much love and acceptance—"

"You don't owe me," he said thickly.

"No. Well, I do, but not in such a merchant-and-buyer kind of way. And it's not supposed to be some kind of balancing scales anyway! What a terrible marriage that would be, constantly checking who owes who—and how do we even decide the weight of an action?"

"But what do we do, then?"

I sighed, laid my head back down on his chest, listened to the plunging roar of his heart. *Purge me with hyssop, and I shall be clean: wash me, and I shall be whiter than snow.* "Thomas, why do you feel guilty about this?"

His hand paused, trembled. "Like I said, there was some responsibility on my part—"

"Did you want it?"

He shifted. "It's complicated! I mean, no, is the easy answer. I didn't—especially at first. But it was...she justified it—and justified it well, sometimes. She was so much like a different person, at first. Not harsh, just that she was misunderstood, or that because she was so passionate about The Beloved it resulted in harsh treatment—"

"You believed her? That how she treated me came from a place of love for The Beloved?"

"No." He was firm about that, and I let out a little sigh. "But other parts of her personality. It did fit. And there was still... I'm not sure how to explain it, but during the little bits of uncertainty, little bits of doubt, I couldn't help that some of the physical pleasure was still there."

"I can't imagine it ever feeling good. That my conscience would still bother me—"

"Well hopefully you never find out." He squirmed out from underneath me and off the bed. I closed my eyes with a frustrated grunt.

"I'm sorry," I said. "That's not the point. Thomas, do you still want it now?"

He paused, head through his tunic but not his arms. He reminded me of a duck and I smiled. "What do you mean?" he asked.

"If Judith were still alive, and let's say I said 'I cannot handle this; leave me and go back to Holden.' Would you go back to Judith?"

His eyes went wide. "Of course not! How can you—?"

"Then why do you still feel guilty? About how you *used* to feel, and only at moments of weakness or whatever it was?"

His arms slowly came through the sleeves. "Well..."

"Did you tell Our Father you were sorry?"

"Yes."

"And you've clearly repented of whatever got you to that point."

"I don't repent of finding you beautiful, and seeking you out wherever you go," he said softly.

I got off the bed and stepped up to him, close, but only gazed into his eyes. "Then why," I said, just as softly. "Do you feel guilty?"

"Because the blood of The Beloved isn't enough to make me clean," he said with a smirk.

"Exactly. So stop it."

"There's one thing you're forgetting," he said, stepping away a pace as he began fastening the laces of his tunic. "I still have visions of Judith, sometimes, when I look at you."

I glanced at him coyly. "I bet the rest of me looks much younger than her."

His eyes went wide, then down to the floor. "Rae-Anna—"

"Shh," I said. "Obviously not right now, we have a murderer to catch. So how do we find out everyone who was awake last night?"

I tried to ignore how relieved he looked as he did up the last lace. He turned away so I could get dressed. "We can't ask them?"

I shook my head resignedly, but began dressing. "Each of them? There are a lot. And we still need a reason as to why we care."

"True. I wonder if Lord Pendrel would have an idea."

"Hmm. But what if it's him?"

Thomas turned slightly toward me. "Surely not? I thought he was away when it happened?"

I shrugged. "So he said. Is it at all possible he somehow came back unknown, and departed again?"

"We could ask his attendants, but no promises they wouldn't just lie for him, if he told them to."

"True." I finished, turning Thomas with a hand on his shoulder and tilting my head for a kiss. He gave it, just as intentionally and tenderly as our wedding day. A little longer this time, too. When he finally stepped back, I smiled. "That should sustain me for a while," I said.

I saw the look on his face, ever so briefly, knew that cursed woman's face had leapt to his mind. Maybe even the words had been hers. I turned away faster than him this time.

"Rae-Anna," he said—almost sobbed.

"No," I said harshly. "I know it's not your fault. I know whose fault it is, and I wish I had cooked her far sooner."

I couldn't imagine he enjoyed hearing such words from me, so I left the room. I needed to get somewhere to think. Some of my best thinking came while I was scrubbing pots in the convent, so as soon as I could I found someone to tell me where the sculleries were. I did quickly ask the servant—she seemed about the same station as the one who had prepared Thomas' and my room when we first arrived—to let Thomas know where I had gone and what I needed.

I walked in, not thinking there would not be many dishes at this hour. A few of the maids startled, then didn't seem to know what to do. I was not royalty, and yet I had sat by their Lord every meal. They finally made rough curtsies, then gazed uncomfortably at me as my eyes burned holes in the empty sinks.

"I just needed to think," I said faintly. "Sometimes washing helps me do that."

"Oh," said one—taller than me, muscled but lean, brown curls tied back tight. She pulled on one of her fingers. "Some platters are sure to be on their way soon. Aren't you missing the meal with his Lordship, though?"

I took a steady breath. "I won't be much use to him this morning," I said. "Slept terribly. I thought I heard some great rattling chain..." I trailed off and my eyes snapped to them. "You didn't hear anything, did you? Or were you still sleeping?"

A few shook their heads. A pale redhead went impossibly paler and swallowed. I turned to her. "What's your name, child?" I asked gently.

Wide green eyes fixed mine. "Laney—Lanette," she said. "They call me Laney."

"Laney. Were you awake, just after midnight?"

"Yes, Miss. But I heard no chains, Miss, promise."

"You heard something else, though?"

She gawked at the other girls. I saw them eyeing her, nervously, saw her begin to stiffen. "Wait," I said quickly. "Come with me, first."

She wiped her hands on her apron, but followed me. As I exited I ran into Thomas, striding hurriedly toward me. "Thomas, not yet, I've—"

"I'm sure, but we have a bigger problem."

I gave him a warning look. "I really must speak to Laney, here, and—" I glanced quickly, and lowered my voice. "I need to do it alone, please."

Thomas folded his arms. "Rae-Anna, the Fool was missing at breakfast. They found his body on the cobblestones just now, below the tower where Mistress Pendrel fell."

Chapter 9

We entered the dining hall amid a flurry of activity. Lord and Lady Pendrel presided at their customary head, but most of the tables and benches had been pushed to the wall. Staff and peasantry alike were in rows in the middle. Of the servants, only Joliff stood apart, still at his master's side. As we came forward he caught our eye, shook his head minutely, then flicked his eyes toward the lines of people.

I paused, swallowed. "I guess we're supposed to stand with them," I said softly to Thomas.

He glanced around, bent to guide me. "Mahmoud is over there."

He stood in a little enclave of those who had also sat at his table. We came near and he saw us, looked us up and down. "I am not sure—"

I waved him off. "Lord Pendrel already knows you, and knows we are friends of yours," I said.

"I fear that may be the problem. We are the newest arrivals, before his court jester is killed. One who made you and Thomas a special target..."

"He jested with everyone—"

"Yes, but he was known to them. You two did not."

I hesitated. "Mahmoud, are you afraid of us being seen with you? Or of you being seen with us?" His uncomfortable silence was answer enough, and I couldn't help but smile. "That doesn't happen to you a lot, does it," I said sadly.

He fixed me with his gaze. "Not in your land. But if we are not imprisoned here, you will soon enter my lands."

My smile faded. "True." I rubbed my eyes. "So, how did you sleep last night?"

He cocked his head. "Well enough, I thank you. What of you?"

I shook my head. "Couldn't sleep. Dragons..." I waved a hand around my head.

"Did you see a murderer?" he asked, but I was distracted by a sudden loud voice.

"You stopped them? Where?" Lord Pendrel said from the dais. He was looking around the hall, and when he saw Thomas and I he frowned. "Thomas and Rae-Anna, come." He waved us up as he said something aside to Joliff, who look chastened.

"I do apologize," Lord Pendrel said as we approached. "Joliff was not wrong to send you away, necessarily. But in this case I want you here. You have heard what happened?"

I nodded. "From Thomas. Not many details though."

Lord Pendrel shook his head. "Terrible. Absolutely terrible. Almost in the exact spot—the exact spot! And the time..."

"Who found him, Lordship?"

"The chandler. It was on his way to his shop."

I furrowed my brow. "Was he also who found—?"

Lord Pendrel nodded emphatically. "He was. Poor man, I may have to move his shop so he can take a different route."

I glanced around the hall, staggered by the sheer number of people. "And now you will question each of these people?" I asked.

"We must! Someone might have seen something, but also I hoped you could listen. Maybe something someone says, or perhaps The Beloved..."

I grinned wryly. "I cannot promise to be a divining rod, Lordship," I said.

"But you two have seemed to know things, since you came here..." He cocked an eyebrow at both of us.

I took a breath. "How did you sleep, your Lordship? Wake up through the night at all?"

He paused, sat back. "I'm...no, not really. But I have never slept well since—well."

"Do you remember what was on your mind? More specifically?"

He stared at me for a time, and I felt as though he were wrestling with how honest and vulnerable to be. He set his jaw as though deciding in favor. "Many things pertaining to my demesne," he said. "I fear I am a poor Lord, too distracted by..." He glanced halfway to Lady Pendrel and back. "Perhaps I worry too much about an heir to leave my estates, than concern for the estates themselves."

I glanced at Thomas. "There are some fields that are struggling—have been for a while," Thomas said. "You worry you let them go too far. Huh. I thought that would have been a farmer, not you."

Lord Pendrel blinked rapidly. "I-I did think that. As to the other: beg pardon?"

"Something happened last night," I said softly. "That we may know who the murderer is—well, we can discover him. Thomas heard his thoughts amid a jumble of others. So he doesn't know who it is, but if we find out what were keeping people awake last night..."

I trailed off, let his Lordship put together the rest. "What we need, is a way to find out who was awake last night without arousing their suspicion."

"I think the way you just did," Thomas said. "Not formally," he hurried on when I squinted. "We'll still have to talk to everyone. But at some point you ask them how they are sleeping—like you just did. I saw you do it twice now, and both people have been forthright in answering you. And then I'll see if I can remember who thought what."

I looked from him to Lord Pendrel, saw agreement in both of their eyes. "I will set it up," Lord Pendrel said. "We'll use a quiet chamber away."

While he turned to confer with Joliff on the arrangements, I turned to Thomas. "Do you think this is the same murderer?" I whispered.

Thomas sighed sadly. "No. I worry the Fool killed her—he was the one who assured Penelope that Mistress Pendrel had returned to her Ladyship—and he killed himself from guilt. But he jumped after I heard his thoughts."

"So what good will this do, then?"

"If none of them are the murderer, then it stands to reason..." He shrugged. "Or I might be wrong."

"This might be a very long day," I said.

Thomas looked over the crowd. "Or two," he agreed.

It was two days, and every bit as painstaking as I feared. It was fortunate to be winter, with little work to do, as no one left the hall except for necessities, and only under guard. I felt like I kept waiting for someone to be shown in, though I could not remember who. As darkness crept on that first day, and it was clear we would not be finished, Lord Pendrel provided pallets for everyone who had not yet been questioned. The more that came and went, the more I was sure the murderer was either not here, was the Fool, or knew better than to admit to sleeping poorly. To that end, Lord Pendrel allowed those questioned who had been cleared by Thomas to return to normal lives. When word of that got out, some who had "forgotten" that they had lain awake were more than happy to come back and share their worries.

I told myself that the shock of the Fool's death was why I had forgotten about Laney until her turn came early the second morning. She entered the small chamber where we had been conducting our questioning, and as soon as she saw me she stepped back, bumping into the guard behind her. He grunted, then shoved her a little too roughly forward.

"No, it's okay," I said quickly to the guard. "Laney, I'm sorry we couldn't talk privately before. I hope you understand why we have to do it this way now."

She nodded, glancing furtively at his Lordship as she sketched a hasty curtsy. "I told you, Miss—and I meant it—"

I held up my hand. "Laney," I said gently. "I can tell something happened. Even if you didn't hear anything, that night meant something to you."

She nodded, still silent.

"Did you see something, instead? You were awake..."

She nodded, started picking at one of her knuckles. "I was awake," she said, her voice almost impossibly small. I leaned forward to try to hear her. "And I saw... It wasn't the first time." She squeezed her eyes shut, shook her head. "I shouldn't have said that."

"Laney, can you tell me what you're afraid of?"

Her eyes went wide as she looked at me, and I noticed the barest flicker of a glance toward his Lordship as she shook her head.

"Lordship," I said hesitantly. I looked at him. "Forgive my impudence, but I must ask if I could talk to her alone."

I could tell it was impudent indeed as his nostrils flared. "I must know what is happening within my demesnes—"

"Lordship, you must realize servants talk about all sorts of things you will never know anything about."

"Of course, so! But if this pertains..."

"I will be sure to tell you, on your word no unnecessary harm will come to her."

Now he truly bristled as he turned to her. "You think me a harsh master, Lanette?"

She shook her head, but a tear slipped down her cheek.

"Lordship, I'm afraid I must insist, as you trust Thomas, myself, and The Beloved," I said. "Please."

I took his silence—however tense—as acceptance. I would not be so impertinent as to ask him to leave, so I rose and guided Laney by the arm out of the room, and to a quiet corner of the hall. Fortunately many had gone already, and a quiet corner existed. I backed myself against the wall to turn her away from the room.

"I'll be sure no one approaches," I said quietly. I glanced across the hall with a strange sense something was still missing. Perhaps it only seemed so empty after that first time we entered. I returned to Laney. "What did you see?"

She glanced behind her once, then to me. "I saw Mistress Pendrel, Miss," she said.

My eyebrows climbed. "Alive?"

She shook her head. "No, of course not. The first time it happened, I almost thought so, and fair shouted for joy. But then Miss Gerty came running and passed right through her mistress so I knew..."

"You've seen her ghost. Since when?"

"The third day after she'd been found dead, Miss."

On the third day she rose again. "Why do you think you see her, and so few others do?"

She shrugged, looking miserable. But not the misery of one who happened into a difficult situation, but one who knew their own fault—or sin?—had brought it to them.

"Laney, you know something about her death, don't you?"

Her face screwed up as she tried not to cry, and shook her head in denial. I sighed, placed a hand on her shoulder. "Laney, you carry this burden for no reason. Unless it was your hand that actually pushed her off the ramparts—"

"No! Of course not, I loved her. She was so kind to all the servants—not a proud bone in her, Miss, only generous. She was such a light. I'd give anything for you to have known her."

"Then tell me what happened."

She told me, haltingly and with a lot of coaxing. The more she talked, the more I knew Lord Pendrel needed to hear it. When she finished, I told her as much. "You know he won't blame you for this," I said.

"But I lied to him—and kept it from him since then. And maybe even let a murderer stay in the castle for years!"

"Has anyone died since then?" I asked.

She shook her head.

"Then it might have still been an accident, or it might have been nothing. Lord Pendrel is wise enough to see that."

"But the lying... I didn't know how it would work out at the time, and I still kept it from him."

I nodded. "Yes, you likely will have to answer for that. But do you think you never will have to answer, now? I'd wager you've punished yourself over it for far longer than Lord Pendrel will." She went silent, but I saw agreement in the set of her jaw, the shame in her eyes. "Laney, this is not your fault. Whether you spoke out or not. We'll tell your tale to Lord Pendrel only in service of the truth—and, I think, of relieving you of an unnecessary burden. All right?"

She nodded, and we went back inside. Thomas sat nearer his Lordship, and both looked over quickly as we entered. Lord Pendrel seemed a little mollified, whatever Thomas might have been saying to him. "Well?" Lord Pendrel asked.

"I think she may shed some light, Lordship, but there will be more to learn afterward."

He sighed. "As I feared. Well, let us hear what you heard—or saw—two nights ago."

"Yes, Lordship. I am sorry, milord, for keeping this from you. I was scared, you see—not just of you, though as you say you've been nothing but fair and that's the truth. But it was such dark days, Lordship. We all felt it."

He sat forward. "Dark days? You do not just mean Thome Fool, do you?"

"No, Lordship, though it concerns him too. The day your daughter—Lordship, I don't need say it. But I overheard Piter—that is, Thome Fool, tell Miss Penelope about Mistress Pendrel, that she'd gone back after her mum—her Ladyship, sir. And I thought nothing of it. It was in passing, Lordship. I was taking some broth to Miss Katherine—you remember she was laid up those days. I put it in her room, and when I came out I saw Thome going aloft, Lordship. Up the ladder to the top of the tower."

Lord Pendrel trembled. "Why did you not say anything?"

"Lordship, I know I should have done! But he went up there so often, you see. 'Tweren't strange. And after—well, Lordship, you looked into it so thoroughly. Everyone accounted for. I thought surely something would have come out if it mattered. And I didn't know if he'd been truthful to Penelope or not, so what difference if he's up there if the Mistress was with her ladyship? It was all so much, and so uncertain, Lordship! When it was all settled I put it out of my mind."

Lord Pendrel scrubbed his forehead. "Yes, of course, I see what you mean. And..." He glanced at me. "I suppose it might have changed nothing. I had never thought Thome capable of it anyway, even if he had been seen for certain on the roof with her. We still don't know why—was he the one you heard then, Thomas?"

Thomas frowned. "It's like I told Rae-Anna, your Lordship: I can't tell. There were so many whispers, and all at once...if it was, he must have gone up afterward. But unless someone saw him, and can verify what time of night..."

"Did you see him again two nights ago?" Lord Pendrel asked Laney.

"No, lordship, I had seen... Sir, I've been seeing Mistress' ghost, sir."

He sat back, eyes wide. "You too?" he breathed. He shook his head. "We thought it was only Lady Pendrel and I. So, why you?"

Laney took a moment to master her trembling lip. "I'm feared, Lordship, it's because I owe her something—that it's my fault she's dead and no one punished, sir."

Lord Pendrel nodded slowly. "Yes. Interesting. But if so, it means the same for her Ladyship and I." He held his hand up quickly to forestall her protests. "No, Lanette, it is only fair. This shall certainly take further looking-into."

"For now, your Lordship," Thomas said, "we have a lot more to question. Nothing is made certain yet."

"We should also look at who you first questioned..." My brow furrowed as I realized who I had been waiting to see. "Lordship, I haven't seen the Archivist."

"Ah, yes. He's so often in his library, perhaps he was forgotten. Joliff, would you fetch him for us please?"

"Of course, Lordship."

Joliff departed and Lord Pendrel turned back to us. "Let us continue anyway, until he arrives. Laney, I will not turn you out, but you understand you have broken a great deal of trust." She nodded, a tear dripping off the end of her nose as she clasped her hands before her. "I will see to it you are put apprentice to the right person, but you cannot remain on the castle staff. Please continue to wait in the hall until someone comes for you."

"Thank you, Lordship," she murmured. It was generous of him, and I think she knew that. But I understood the difficulty too. Apprenticeship was less certain, especially under the cloud of displeasing his Lordship. But she turned and went, her head a little higher at least.

"It will still be hard for her, Lordship," I said quietly as we waited for the next to be questioned.

He sighed. "Only for a time. I will make sure of it." He fixed me with his gaze. "I wonder though if she was the only one who knew she held something back."

"Do you think the Fool did it, Lordship? That he killed himself in remorse?"

Lord Pendrel shook his head. "Why now? Just because the two of you arrived?"

"Has the dragon been this active before?"

He nodded sagely. "That is a fair question, young maiden. He has not. I wonder why?"

Thomas smirked. "We seem to have that effect, Lordship."

Three more came and went, of no help. Only one had been awake, and had again been worried about personal things. Thomas shook his head, and the minor servant was dismissed.

"What is taking Joliff so long?" Lord Pendrel mused. "The archives are not so far—"

We were interrupted by loud protests from outside, someone who did not want to be brought in. Thomas bolted upright at the sound of his voice. Lord Pendrel noticed immediately.

"Guards! Bring that man!" he bellowed.

Just as the doors opened, between the wrestling hands of the guards I saw the man we had seen near the broken scaffolding when we arrived. His eyes were wild, and I saw a glint of steel near the armpit of the guard on the left. "Look out!" I shouted, nearly on top of Thomas.

Too late, the blade plunged. As the guard cried out, the man wrenched free and ran. The second guard chased him as the first slumped to the floor. "Stop him!" Lord Pendrel shouted.

The guards near the door lowered their halberds, and the man impaled himself on both. I turned quickly away from the sight, though the sounds of his death still reached me—and reach me still. I could not follow the clamor that ensued, between Lord Pendrel, his guards, and those still left in the hall.

I did not come to myself until the sound cut off abruptly, and I heard Joliff's voice asking: "Lordship?"

I turned. Joliff stood in the doorway to the hall, understandably bewildered. Lord Pendrel looked at him, then past him.

"Joliff," Lord Pendrel said. "Where—?"

"He's not there, Lordship. And his key is on his desk."

We all stared at each other, now each as bewildered as Joliff.

Chapter 10

We all stood in the Archives, glancing around, still bewildered. Thomas and I had only spent a few days in the room, but Favish had been such a constant presence that, without him there, it seemed we shouldn't really move until he returned.

Lord Pendrel finally cleared his throat, and with it seemed to banish whatever spell was on us. We passed through the stacks of books, as though perhaps Joliff had only missed him crouched down looking for some ancient tome. But it was too silent. I could tell he was no longer there.

Somehow we all made our way back to the main table at the same time. We exchanged glances, then looked together at the table where his key lay. We let the silence breathe a few moments. It seemed his memorial.

"But where did he go?" Lord Pendrel muttered, voicing the question for all of us.

"And did he kill the Fool?" Thomas asked next.

Lord Pendrel looked at us. "And what does Amaury have to do

with all of this?"

I had nearly forgotten when I couldn't remember his name. "The man who ran in the hall? He was a journeyman mason, Captain Boris said?"

Lord Pendrel grimaced. "He showed some promise. Did you see the newest wall when you arrived, as Boris brought you to the keep? Yes. It saved many lives when the scaffolding beside it collapsed. Including...well, our daughter was somewhat nearby, and might have been injured. Or crushed."

Thomas frowned. "His speech pattern reminded me of the murderer in my dream," he said.

"How would that be?" Pendrel asked.

Thomas shook his head, looking over the table. "I have no idea. But when he came in, a sense washed over me that when we questioned him, I would hear the words that came to me. As if it had already happened, I already knew. I would have liked to hear him actually say it though. Just to be sure..."

Lord Pendrel sighed. "I thought this was sealed," he muttered. "I had searched, questioned... Everything fit, at least as far as we could ascertain. But now..."

"Lordship, are we sure the Fool was not up on the roof with her when she fell?" I asked.

"Nothing seems certain anymore."

"Why were you certain back then?"

"I suppose perhaps I was not. But he had served my father—he and I practically grew up together. So when he looked me in the eye and said he was not there, I saw no duplicity. I simply believed him." He shook his head. "I still don't know if I believe it."

"Something is still wrong here," Thomas said. "Why is Favish's key here? Why would he leave it?"

"Perhaps so whoever took his place would have it."

"You could make a new one, I'd wager, with little trouble. And if he was set to murder the Fool, it seems an odd bit of conscience."

Joliff entered, then, and approached Lord Pendrel. He whispered in his ear before stepping respectfully away. "Lady Pendrel is in a state," Lord Pendrel said heavily. He shook his head sadly. "Of course. I'm stupid sometimes. She would have thought this all closed up too. You two stay here and see if you can find anything. I'll send Joliff when I'm ready."

As he left, I looked at Thomas. "What are we supposed to do?" I wondered aloud.

"Look around, I guess."

I shrugged, looking at the table. There were a few books across it, some loose papers. I looked through them, scanning their titles and a few lines from the pages. But they were haphazard, and I could discern no link between what they were about. Odd, I thought. Favish had seemed better-organized than that. Had he been interrupted? But during what?

Thomas moved off to the stacks again, and I could hear him humming to himself. "Rae-Anna?" he called. I sensed no urgency in his voice, so I merely responded.

"Yes, love?"

He was silent for a time. "Is that what you're going to call me?"

I smiled. "You don't like it?" I looked at the few chairs around the table to see if some other piece of archive had fallen there, but they were empty.

"I guess I'm not... I don't know. It doesn't feel right, I guess."

I stood, looking off to the direction he had gone though I couldn't see him. A strange sense washed across me, not quite nausea. "Love doesn't feel right?"

"I don't mean that... That's weird. Favish wouldn't have candles just lit randomly throughout these books would he?"

"I can't imagine. What *did* you mean, then?"

"Oh, I guess just that you've called me 'Thomas' for so long. Did you find anything over there?"

I chewed my lip, made a cursory glance though I had searched thoroughly already. "No. Just random papers. You know Saint Paul changed his name after he became enamored of The Beloved."

Thomas laughed, and the unease returned, much stronger. "So shouldn't I choose whether I want to change my name or not, then?"

I swallowed, and the nausea colored to anger. "So I shouldn't be surprised if you don't want to change your name, then."

Thomas leaned out from a row of shelves. "What?"

I glared at him. "Well I did say Paul was enamored of The Beloved when he changed his name."

He stepped out fully, then, folding his arms. "Do you remember that this all started because I was about to ask you a question?"

I blinked as the nausea faded. "Oh right. What is it?"

Thomas, I could tell, barely kept from rolling his eyes. "Actually, I wanted to ask you if you meant it when you said you wished you had...what happened to Judith had happened earlier."

I pulled out a chair and sat heavily. "I don't know. Maybe not as harshly as I said it, but..."

"Because of what happened to me, or because of how it's affecting you now?"

I rubbed my forehead. "That's a very fine line—"

"But an important one."

It was, and I knew it. I just didn't want to say it, not that baldly. But did it truly matter? Was my desire less pure just because I wanted it for me as well? He started to turn away. "Don't you walk away from me, Thomas," I said. All of it was unfair—to him, to me. He turned back in surprise. I felt something like a soft breeze at my back, pushing my emotions forward though they made me sick. "Do you think I care about you so little? Of course it would still matter to me! Were I still stuck in the convent and you still a farmer. Maybe I wouldn't be as mad, maybe I wouldn't wish such a terrible fate—but I think I might still want as definitive a fate to befall her even if all I knew of you was your name and the crime she had committed."

"The other Sisters didn't seem to. What if you had become—"

I bolted to my feet. "How dare you! Thomas of Holden do you think so little of me? What made you marry me if that's all you think? If it was how I looked in Tabitha's dress she made for me, we can go give it back right now—I'll have nothing to do with you if that's what you want!"

We stared at each other. "That easy, is it?" he said with dangerous quiet.

"Our Father help us," I groaned, sitting back down. "Thomas, you cannot treat me this way. I am truly sorry you can't seem to pull me close, but don't push me away either and make it seem like it's my fault."

He lowered his gaze, picked at a fingernail. "I never should have..."

"Fine. Yes. We never should have. How far back do you want to go, by the way? Never married me? Never left Holden? Never stuck around after I revealed the Fire? Never come to the convent? Never thought I was pretty? Never watched me lean over a horse stall? Never saw me in the first place? Maybe I shouldn't have been born—would that be far back enough?" My voice went suddenly deep as I said: "when does the regret start?" I stared at him, hand over my mouth. I felt I needed to clear my throat. The Fire inside was cold—or, it burned brightly, but behind a veil of ice and snow. The breeze I had felt at my back had returned, frigid and stiff, washing over me like putrid breath.

Thomas had leaped forward, was shouting something I couldn't hear. He grabbed my arm and yanked me away from the chair. Noise returned as my slippered feet skittered across the stone floor. I turned back and could see something like blue smoke pouring over the seat where I had been sitting. I glanced up, but wherever it had originated had cut it off. It drifted to the floor, billowing outward. Just as it reached my toe I felt the same nausea, the same anger and bitterness. I called out this time and the Fire burned it back.

"When did that start?" I asked, relieved my voice had returned to normal.

Thomas clutched me, still, and was pressing his face into my neck. "I'm so sorry," he said. "I'm sorry I'm making this so hard for you. It's not fair. We are supposed to share one another's burdens, not dump them on each other entirely. I've been horrible—"

"Thomas, shush. I've been unfair to you, too. Though now I wonder..." I paused as something under my chair glittered. I hadn't noticed it when it was pushed under the table. "Thomas, what is that?"

He looked over. "What?"

"I didn't see—Sorry." I kissed him quick on the cheek as I extricated myself from his—shall we say, urgent embrace. I went over and looked. "It's..." I almost couldn't believe it. And when I pulled it out, I saw in front of it, pushed even further under the table, the rest. I pulled out all the articles and held them up.

"Favish's clothing?" Thomas said, his voice the embodiment of my own confusion.

"What was the candle you found earlier?" I asked.

Thomas stared, then shook his head. "Oh it wasn't the candle. A piece of wax, though, had dripped on the floor. I thought he would have been more careful with a candle, is all."

"Show me," I said, dropping the clothes onto a chair.

He led me around, and I glanced at the books across the shelves. There was a small gap between two of the books. I put a finger in it, quickly read the spines of the books on either side. "From here," I muttered. I went back to the table. "Find me a piece of paper and a quill," I said, glancing over the books again. I studied the loose papers—surely they had not been shelved. So why—? Thomas brought me the implements, and I quickly copied the names of the books.

"What is it?" Thomas asked.

"Favish, for some reason, was hurriedly gathering these books. But they don't seem to relate—look. *Pruning Ones Gardens*—their actual gardens, it's not a metaphor. *Reading DeChambeau,* he was a historian, I think. *Illustrations for Life,* something like Proverbs. *Troubadours Ballads,* even? Why these? And this one: *Enter the Night!* it's...unless it refers to his murderer or kidnapper somehow." I shrugged. "Anyway, it was the one missing from where you saw the wax dripping. But it's fiction, a story about a young man foundering in his work, trying and failing as an apprentice."

"How do you know about that one?" Thomas asked.

"Oh. Um. I wasn't supposed to read it." I copied the last title, then moved back into the rows of shelves.

"Why weren't you supposed—what is it, more wax?"

"Yes," I said, staring at it. Had he dripped it on purpose? Or did it slosh as he searched for the exact book? Again there was nothing in the gap where he had pulled it from. I moved on. "The Sisters didn't think it was fit for a young woman to read."

"Well, was it?"

"No, it wasn't. I should have listened. Here it is again, right below where he took it from. But why?" I stared at the paper, trying to make sense.

Thomas was beside me, picking at one of the spines absent-mindedly. "What was it, bad words? Like curses or something?"

I looked blankly at him. "Oh. Thomas, no. For—" I shook my head. "I've forgotten most of it, I promise. And I really don't think that was why Favish picked them, anyway. I don't know if their contents...actually..." I trailed off. Did their contents matter? Or maybe he had put something inside the books themselves—I almost started back, except he had dripped wax at each place. That could not have been a coincidence.

"I just don't want you to have the wrong idea about... I mean, the wrong expectations for what I can do..."

"What? Thomas!" I hit my thigh with the hand that was holding the paper. "I'm really not thinking about that right now, please? Can we focus on what's going on here?"

"Fine. Give it." He snatched the paper from my hand and looked over it.

"Thomas, we've only just begun teaching you—"

"It's his name," he said abruptly.

"What is?"

He handed me the paper. "I know I can't read it all yet, but I know most of the letters, and I know the name 'P-I-T-E-R' when I see it, even if they're jumbled."

He was right. In the right order, the first letter of each title spelled the name Piter. "But...who is...?"

"Thome Fool. Remember Laney called him Piter? Probably was his real name. And Favish wanted us to know it was Piter, without Piter being able to tell. And that the books weren't random, which was why he dripped wax at each place. There would be too many co-incidences, if someone looked. And strange as this room is, someone would have looked eventually."

"So where is he then? Why isn't he here?"

Thomas shrugged, then froze. "Oh, I might know. Come with me, in case I'm wrong."

Without thinking, I brought the paper with me as I followed Thomas through the halls. Eventually we found Joliff. "Are we able to see his Lordship?" Thomas asked.

Joliff paused only briefly before turning and leading us. "You did not find the Archivist?" he asked.

"Perhaps," Thomas said.

Joliff regarded him with a raised brow, then looked at me. Since Thomas wasn't ready, I didn't say anything either. "Very well," Joliff muttered.

He quickly brought us to an upper chamber. "Wait here." He ducked inside, returning shortly with Lord Pendrel behind him.

"How is her Ladyship?" I asked in reflex. "Was she able to calm down from the uproar?"

Lord Pendrel scoffed. "It was not, unfortunately, just the uproar. Apparently Zimón the Chandler had begun regaling the hall with his tale. He was…most vivid in his details."

"Who all saw the body?" Thomas asked.

"Zimón, obviously. Myself. Boris."

"And you all could see it was Thome?"

Lord Pendrel frowned. "Well of course it was, he was wearing his garb. And we had been looking for him—"

"I'm sorry, Lordship, but could you see for certain it was him? His face?"

Lord Pendrel went white, but mastered himself. "I'm afraid that was more difficult," he said hoarsely. Joliff handed him a cup of water, which he drank quickly. "He had fallen on his head. There was not much of it left." His eyes went hard. "Which is why Lady Pendrel was so put out—that daft chandler..." He looked at us, and I looked at Thomas.

"It wasn't him, was it?" I breathed.

"Well then who—" Lord Pendrel's eyes went wide. "You mean to say it was Favish?"

"How did he get his clothes, though?" I asked, still mostly to Thomas.

"Favish was not a weak man," Thomas said. "But I wonder if Thome was threatening him with something."

"But then why not just kill the Fool? Why kill himself?" Lord Pendrel demanded.

I could tell by Thomas' blank stare he didn't know. "That may come, yet," I said. "But that still leaves Thome missing."

Lord Pendrel groaned. "I would rather Favish was missing—he was not so clever at hiding as Thome was."

"Has he not fled the castle?"

Lord Pendrel rubbed his jaw. "He wouldn't have to, that one. He knows every bolt-hole and nook in all Fosse. Probably has food and drink hidden away somewhere and will wait out while we search, then slip off when we've given up."

"Why not just leave immediately?"

"To drive us mad, of course." Lord Pendrel waved his hand. "Perhaps I am only weary and angry. Joliff, tell Boris and have him begin a search. For all the good it might do." Joliff bowed and moved off. "You two...do whatever it is you do, I suppose. I must attend her Ladyship for some little time, yet."

"Yes, Lordship," we chorused. He returned to his room, and I turned to Thomas. "What is next for us?" I asked.

Thomas shrugged. "That was all I'd put together so far."

"He asked a very important question," I said, nodding toward the closed door.

"Why Favish killed himself and left clues for Piter? Yeah. Let's work on that, I guess."

"Where?"

"The archives. There's still something about this timeline that isn't working."

Chapter 11

"Where are we starting?" I asked as we entered the archives once again.

Thomas picked up the clothes I had left on the chair and moved them to a small vacant shelf. He paused a moment as he looked at them, and I thought perhaps he mouthed a prayer. He rubbed his eyes. "Well," he began, returning to the table, "we assume this has something to do with the dragon, right? The one that has always been here but didn't seem to appear until a specific moment. Have we figured out when that moment was? Or who saw it first?"

"Lady Pendrel and I were interrupted when I asked her. But she was far down the road of not knowing—she mentioned that it looked so much like what you would think the dragon of Fosse would look like, that you would think you had to have seen it before."

Thomas' eyes narrowed. "What does it look like to you?" he asked.

I shrugged helplessly. "A dragon. Dark scales, wide wings, glittering eyes."

"And carries memories like jewels."

"Right."

"Were there any memories you saw in there that weren't ours?"

I thought back, tried to remember. "There were many, but I only actually focused on a few," I said uncertainly.

Thomas snorted. "And one of them wasn't even yours..." He sobered. "Interesting, isn't it? That of all the memories he held, that was the one you saw clearest."

"Maybe not—because it wasn't mine, it caught my attention. Because it didn't fit with the rest."

"But also perfectly chosen to make you doubt our relationship."

"Do you think that's what the dragon does, then? Drive people apart?"

Thomas shrugged. "It certainly does that, whether that's its intention or not. Doesn't tell us how to get rid of it, though."

I leaned forward on folded arms, looking at the books and papers still scattered across the table. "And it doesn't explain why Mistress Pendrel's ghost still walks the ramparts." I found myself scanning some of the papers again as I mused. "Ghosts aren't a regular thing. Right? As I mentioned to Favish, even in the Holy Words I can only think of one instance where someone consulted a medium—and even then, the ghost was specifically called up. It didn't just wander. Ignoring a lot of folklore about ghosts, it doesn't make sense."

"What if we don't ignore the folklore?"

I eyed him a moment. "Then we stray from the Words, and The Liar has his way with us."

"So someone is calling her up, specifically?"

I grunted. "I wonder. There were a few who seemed like they would. Both Pendrels, for one. Laney spoke, too, of wishing I could meet her."

Thomas cocked an eyebrow. "Favish?"

My eyebrows flared, then furrowed as I continued to read what was in front of me. "Do you know what I didn't do? I was so focused on the books laid out here, I didn't bother with the papers. They seem just as random, but they wouldn't necessarily be, would they?"

"What are they about?"

"Well, this one seems to be notes on crop rotations—specific ones, how they had moved them one year. It's under the heading of trying to get the land to yield the most with various crops."

Thomas shrugged. "My father had some of those, too. It's only good farming."

Despite his assurance, I kept reading. "It mentions Joliette."

"Why?"

"I guess he was making the observations from on the tower. She was there."

"Who's 'he'?"

I glanced across the page. "It doesn't say, but I think Favish wrote this. It feels more personal than historical."

"Well, we knew she went up there a lot. Anything else?"

I quickly read the rest, and shook my head. I pulled the next toward me and read. "This is his too."

"I guess that makes sense, why they're not bound in a book. They must be personal notes."

"Hmm. Even more telling that these are the ones that are laid out, too. This is about a dinner his Lordship held one night." I looked up. "Was Favish at any of the dinners we've had since we were here?"

Thomas paused, considering. "If he was, he snuck in. I tended to be focused on the Pendrels; they conversed with us the most."

"I don't remember either. But he was at this one. Mistress Pendrel, again. Apparently she was fidgeting and was sent away. Huh. But the roast duck was delicious." I shook my head. Thomas handed me the next and I read. Halfway through I stopped, picked up the last and scanned it. "Each one of these is about something entirely different, but Mistress Pendrel is in each one almost as an aside. She just happened to be there, and he made a quick observation."

"But he must have picked these specifically, right? So he went through and found whatever notes he had that had observations of her in them."

"Okay?"

"Well, it just means it's not *that* strange—it just seems strange laid out this way. So if we ignore what seems strange about it, what does it tell us?"

"He's trying to tell us about her. Taking them along with the books as hints, that she was tied up somehow with Piter."

"That he killed her?"

I hesitated. "Well, Favish might have thought so. Maybe. I don't see proof here, though. And I thought the murderer was the man who impaled himself earlier?"

"The murderer of Joliette. We don't know if anyone murdered Favish, or if he threw himself off, or what happened to Piter."

I let out a frustrated sigh and shook my head. "Or if everyone is trapped here, including us, and why."

"We never did ask Mahmoud about that."

"You know, when we saw him in the hall he made a comment about being imprisoned here. Not that he was," I continued quickly as Thomas' eyes widened. "He said if we are not imprisoned here, we would soon see his lands."

"He did, didn't he? But Lord Pendrel called us up before we could talk much further. Would he have assumed we would be that strongly suspected?"

I shrugged. "Or that he would. This whole time we thought he would be safe, because he seemed so well known. I wonder, though: being well known does not always mean well-liked."

"We need to talk to him again."

We rose, and for some reason I straightened all the papers and books before we left. I worried for Mahmoud, though, how the perception of his people might open him to judgements the rest of us weren't open to. And I felt a stirring, deep inside, that I would indeed soon see it from the other side—that I would be cast under immediate suspicion just because of my fair skin, and perhaps because of my scars.

I shook it off, though, as we made our way back to the main halls to find Mahmoud. *Take therefore no thought for the morrow: for the morrow shall take thought for the things of itself. Sufficient unto the day is the evil thereof.* So far, Our Father had given us what gifts we needed to face the trials of the day—if we chose not to receive them, that was our failing, not His. *So what gift do we need today, to face this dragon?*

But many ancient men, that had seen the first house, when the foundation of this house was laid before their eyes, wept with a loud voice; and many shouted aloud for joy.

Sometimes, the Fire gave me things I did not find as helpful as He did. Thomas glanced back at me.

"Maybe Castle Fosse isn't as prosperous as it was before the current Lord Pendrel took over," he said.

I stared at him, then smiled as I shook my head. "I keep forgetting sometimes He speaks to us both at the same time. Fosse seems very prosperous now, though."

Thomas grinned. "Which is why the younger shout aloud with joy," he said. "To those who remember nothing, a loaf of bread with some fish and wine is a feast. To those with roast duck..."

"Something else to ask his Lordship when we can—Joliff!" I

called, spying him scurrying across the hall. "Mahmoud's room?"

He peered at us. "Servants quarters," he said brusquely. "Lower hall, east wing."

"Joliff, how well is Mahmoud known to you?"

He glanced away as though he needed to leave, but laced his fingers together as he turned toward us. "He has passed through many times. I believe he has provided his Lordship with some items from the Silk Road, on occasion."

"Hard to find items?" I asked. "His Lordship has no other place to get them."

Joliff spread his hands. "We are still a remote castle—important, but out of the way. Few pass through."

"I'm sure if too many came through, they would take advantage of his Lordship's largesse," I said with a smile.

Joliff hesitated. "Indeed."

"It is—I'm sorry." I glanced worriedly at Thomas. "I don't want to presume. We are most indebted to their Lord and Ladyship for keeping us through the winter. I don't deny it. But...I'm sorry, we never spoke of it of course. It wouldn't be tactful." I lowered my voice. "And yet, with The Beloved's call on us, it would help us to know if that debt should be paid."

I saw a bit of a haunted look in Joliff's eyes for just a moment, but he quickly covered it by wiping his brow. "Yes, of course, I understand. One could never bring it up to his Lordship. But of course in your situation..." He smiled through his fluster, quickly clasped his hands behind his back. "His Lordship will exact no payment from you, I'm sure. Especially, if you remove the curse of the dragon from us—I would think that would more than make up for a few meals at his Lordship's table."

"Ah. Yes, I suppose. Thank you. But, Joliff... Are there others who do not have the benefit of our position, who perhaps have a debt too large to pay back?"

He cleared his throat, and his forearms wriggled in a way that I thought his fingers must be fluttering furiously behind his back. "I don't know all of his Lordship's debts or credits, certainly. Nor how he considers one paid and another not. But he is fair—has he not been fair to all you've seen? And I trust him."

I nodded vigorously. "Very true, Joliff. Forgive me: his Lordship indeed seems most fair." I pointed quickly. "Lower hall, east wing?"

He smiled with relief. "Yes, he should be there. He does not often move around the halls except for meal times. We will see you tonight?"

"Yes, most definitely. Hopefully we will have more information for his Lordship as well, tonight."

His eyes widened. "Have you discovered something in the Archives?"

I held a finger to my lips, then gestured to the walls. "They have ears," I said, lightly even though I meant it seriously. And there was too much we didn't know—I didn't know if our suspicions alone would satisfy his Lordship, or frustrate him as much as they did us. I looked to Thomas, who turned and made his way down the hall. I gave a small departing wave to Joliff, who seemed to come to himself as he suddenly strode off on his original course as well.

"Well that would be a reason Mahmoud isn't trapped here," Thomas said.

I shrugged noncommittally. "It would be if Lord Pendrel himself is holding people here. I can't get the sense that he is—at least not personally. As Joliff said, he has seemed very fair so far."

"Hmm. Almost too fair, wouldn't you say?"

"Go on."

"Well, what if it's a guilty conscience? People are trapped—he knows they're trapped, and it's his fault but he can't do anything about it. So as an apology for trapping them here, he at least lets them feast in his hall every night through the winter."

We turned down the next hallway. "So then why isn't Mahmoud trapped? Why do I feel like we aren't trapped?"

Thomas gave an exaggerated shrug. "That's what we need to find out."

"On top of where Piter is, why Favish killed himself, who killed Mistress Pendrel, and why the dragon is here."

Thomas paused before the door to the servants quarters. "They might all be related," he said quietly. "Perhaps the dragon is keeping them here. And the only way to leave is to die."

I stared at him. "Very dramatic, Thomas. Thank you."

He cocked an eyebrow. "As dramatic as being trapped in spelled armor by a biblical demon?"

"And as dramatic as raising a bunch of friars from the dead to kill the Sisters. Fair enough." I smiled grimly, then gestured him to open the door.

When we entered, we found Mahmoud kneeling on a prayer rug. I placed a hand on Thomas' arm and pointed him quietly off to the side. As we waited, I offered my own prayers, felt in the Fire inside that Thomas did the same. As time went on, I felt as though a fly had come into the room, though of course no flies would be in the air in winter. Mahmoud, I saw, seemed disturbed. His prayers faltered occasionally, or he seemed to lose his place. Finally he turned and looked at us—almost glared, though the heat in his glance I can't say came from him. But I did not whisper or mutter, only watched in a sort of fascination the prayer rituals of another. And so, with a sigh, he seemed to end his prayers, rose, and rolled up his rug. He turned toward us.

"You came to me?" he asked.

"We didn't meant to disturb you," I said. "I tried to stay off in the corner—"

He cut me off with a wave. "I know. You and Thomas both have been respectful. Thank you." I smiled, though he still did not. "What do you want?"

"We wondered about your relationship with Castle Fosse—the Pendrels, and the others here."

"I am a merchant," he said. "And yet..." He gestured around the quarters.

"You're treated as a servant," I said. "Why do you come back?"

I saw the ghost of a smile on his lips. "I am not paid as a servant."

"How long have you been coming through Fosse?"

He glanced away uncertainly. "Ten years. More." He shrugged.

"Before the current Lord Pendrel reigned?"

"Yes."

I glanced at Thomas. "Was it better, before? More prosperous, or more..."

"It was the same."

"Has it deteriorated? Gotten worse since he took over?"

"I am not here as much as you think. I cannot say."

I paused, considering whether to ask the next question. "You said earlier, when we were in the hall, that we would soon see your country if we were not imprisoned. Why did you think we might be?"

His eyes glittered as he glanced between us. "They did not know you. And we had soon come, and knew things you should not know. It surprises me they do not suspect you."

"Mahmoud, you knew in Aurden that something was wrong. Does anything here seem wrong—except that a dragon is appearing along with the ghost of a girl who died some time ago?"

"Eight years."

My eyes widened. "Eight years? You know that?"

"Of course. Nine years ago I came, she was here. The next year..." He waved his fingers in a drifting-away motion.

"Why does no one else seem to want to remember it exactly?" I mused. "Do you know when the dragon appeared?"

He shook his head as Thomas answered: "He doesn't see him."

"Still. Odd. Isn't it, Thomas? Did his Lordship ever give you an exact date—or at least year—that Mistress Pendrel died?"

He shook his head. "I always thought it was more recent, though."

"Favish said something about the ghost appearing last year, and for everyone else the grief seemed so recent..."

Thomas nodded. "They talk as though they are only now moving on from it."

"Are they trapped here? In the castle?" I asked suddenly, turning to Mahmoud.

His mouth gaped, but I saw no recognition or subterfuge in his eyes. "I am not," he said. "I cannot say—there are not many who would leave a stronghold. Especially..." He gestured around.

"One so far away from everything. True enough." I chewed my lip. "And why wouldn't the Lord and Lady produce another heir?" I snorted. "I say another; they didn't truly have a first." I glanced again at Mahmoud. "Servants can be very talkative," I suggested.

"I have heard little," he replied. "As you say, they seem to only be getting over the loss."

"Is that what the servants say?"

Mahmoud clasped his hands behind his back. "One said perhaps they cannot. She was silenced immediately."

"Which one?"

"I believe she was called Lanette."

"Laney," I breathed, shaking my head. "That cannot be coincidence. I wonder if she is already gone."

"She gathered her things not long ago," Mahmoud said.

"Really? We might catch her before she leaves. Thank you Mahmoud!" I called as I pushed Thomas ahead of us and we scurried down the corridors. "Do you think she knew? Or why would she be the only one to think so?"

"Or did they tell her to be quiet because they thought it too?"

I shook my head. "Lady Pendrel did show great concern for being the proper lady. She would hide something like that, I think. But for how long? His Lordship still needs an heir some way."

Thomas only shook his head. We reached the main entrance, saw the back of Laney between two guards as they escorted her through a sally port. "Wait!" we shouted, almost in unison.

All three turned, and one of the guards—recognizing us—laid a hand on Laney's shoulder. He guided her back between them to stand before us. I smoothed my hair as I tried to catch my breath.

"May we take her just over there?" Thomas asked. "We need to ask her something privately, but I understand you need to make sure she leaves."

"Of course, Thomas."

We took her aside, her eyes filled with questions. "Laney," I said with a quick glance at the guards. "Mahmoud mentioned you said something, once, that perhaps her Ladyship was not able to bear more children."

Her eyes went wide. "I meant nothing by it, Miss; of course her Ladyship is most wonderful—"

"Laney," I said quickly. "Do you think we're trying to bring you more trouble?"

She took a steadying breath. "No, Miss."

"So. Why did you say that?"

"Well, it made sense, Miss. His Lordship needs an heir, and they haven't one. It seemed strange enough to me that they only had Mistress Pendrel anyway. Unless his Lordship wanted the demesne to go to someone else, but I've not heard anything. I'm not acquainted with grief like her Ladyship, Miss, that's the truth of it. But...well don't they need another one?"

"Why do you think the other servants hushed you?" Thomas asked.

"I did speak out of turn, sir. It wasn't right for me to bring it up. Penelope, maybe, or Piter—"

"Piter?"

"He was uncanny, that one was. Knew things he shouldn't have known. And he could show up places— Once I left him in the kitchen to take some soup to Janice—she was laid up; I'm usually the one who takes care of them's laid up..." She trailed off, her lip quivering. "I *was*..."

"I'm sorry, Laney, truly. But you were saying?"

"Right. Sorry. My own fault, his Lordship's got the right of it. Well, I took the fastest way I knew—cold soup's no good to anyone who's laid up—but when I got there Piter was already inside halfway through a tumbling routine! I've no idea how he got there, or so fast."

"Maybe he ran?"

"He would have to pass me, sir. No, that Piter, he knew the secret ways. And he used them to listen in where he shouldn't. It was him as told us his Lordship sometimes surprised her Ladyship being back in the castle when we all thought he was gone."

"When was this? When Mistress Pendrel had fallen?"

"Oh, he did that many a time. But nothing recently."

"Eight years ago?"

She tapped her chin. "I think he was still doing it then." She snapped her fingers. "Now you mention it, Piter was there when I said that fool thing about her Ladyship. And he had just been telling us about one of his Lordship's surprises." She shrugged. "Like I said, nothing so recent—"

"Laney, Mistress Pendrel died eight years ago."

Her eyes went wide. "Was it? It doesn't seem...where does the time go?"

The guard motioned to us. "Madam, I hate to intrude, but..."

"No, that's fine," I said quickly. "She was very helpful. Thank you, Lanette."

She gave us a somber smile and followed the guard to the postern.

"We need to find Piter," I said to Thomas. "And maybe his Lordship as well."

Chapter 12

"Do you have a plan?" Thomas asked as we retraced our steps back toward the archives.

"Favish showed us almost everything else," I said. "I'm hoping he left us a few more clues."

We reached the doors to find two guards posted there. "You're new," I said.

"Yes ma'am," said one.

"Are we allowed to pass?"

They glanced at each other. "Of course," he said. "You're the only ones."

I raised my brows. "Why just us?"

He shrugged. "Just our orders, ma'am. From his Lordship." He turned the latch and opened the door for us.

I cocked an eyebrow at Thomas as we went inside. I stopped when the guards pulled the door shut behind us. "Do you think we should be worried?"

He shrugged. "About what?"

I glanced at the door. "That's our only way out."

"Then you better figure out what your plan is."

I rolled my eyes as I continued toward the table. "Like I said, I don't really have—" I stopped short. The books and papers were laid out on the table again. "Who did that?"

"Guards!" Thomas called. The door open and one of them peered in, halberd gripped tightly. "Did you do this?" Thomas asked, gesturing. The guard stared blankly at the table, then at Thomas.

"No, sir," he said honestly.

"Thank you." The guard pulled his head back and shut the door. Thomas looked them over, then back at me. "Well, there's your clue."

"Is it?"

"Doesn't it have to be? I mean, if I'm not mistaken, they're laid out exactly like they were before."

I looked again. It did seem so. "But what does it—"

"It's a map," he said. "Look, the books are laid out the way we found them in the stacks. So that end is that side of the library, this end is the doors."

"What are the papers?"

He studied them, looked at the shelves, glanced up at the ceiling. Frowned. "I'm not sure." I saw his eyes flickering, trying to take it all in as he thought.

"Don't be afraid to ask the Fire," I said quietly. "Or, the Seed, I guess."

He flashed me a grin. "I am. It's sort of helping?" He shook his head. "It must be nice to just have Him speak directly to you."

"Not really. It's still not always clear. Like what He said earlier about the older ones weeping while the younger rejoiced."

"I would still rather have that. For me, it's like ten different sayings and I've got to see how they connect to each other. And it's not like

He's speaking—they're sort of written on the branches of a plant. And depending on how I look at the plant, the order I come to each stem and leaf, they connect in a different order..." He trailed off as his eyes went wide. "Oh." He moved closer to the books, traced with his finger the books in the order that would spell out P-I-T-E-R. "Parchment and quill," he mumbled, quickly grabbing the few things from where I had left them. He traced the pattern, then connected the papers in the order they would have been written in. He grinned, then showed me the paper.

There was one spot where both sets of lines crossed. He strode to the place, near the shelves but not among them. I followed more slowly. He looked up, then down. "Ah," he said. I came alongside him as he knelt to tug on the bars of a grate. I expected the screech of metal against stone, but instead it swung up easily. Faintly in the hole I could see a few iron rungs leading downward.

"Bring a light," he said, tossing the parchment aside.

"Are you sure we won't need that?" I asked.

He hesitated, then looked up at me. *"If I make my bed in hell, behold, thou art there. But He's also writing: Judge not, and ye shall not be judged: condemn not, and ye shall not be condemned...For a good tree bringeth not forth corrupt fruit."* He shrugged. "So, do with that what you will."

"I will hope He writes that to you to say Piter is not evil," I said as I moved off to find a lantern. I found one, empty, fixed a rushlight in it, and returned.

"Are you sure that will be enough?" Thomas asked.

"I don't think Piter is sitting in the pitch dark hoping someone finds him."

"Unless he's not alive down here."

"In which case we wouldn't be able to judge or condemn him, and your Seed wouldn't bother with that particular leaf. Go, I'm right above you."

Thomas grinned and shook his head as he sat on the edge and gripped the rungs. He descended slowly, allowing me to catch up and keep up with only one hand while the other held the lantern. The hole was small enough for me to brace my back when I needed to rest my muscles. And it was shallow enough I only had to do so once before we reached the bottom.

It was deathly silent down in that buried hall. It ran in only one direction, and was only wide enough for me to hold the lantern to light Thomas' way. Despite the assurance of The Vine, he had his sword drawn as we made our way along the passage. The air grew colder as we walked, and I nearly began to shiver. We turned, and Thomas pressed a hand against the stones.

"Freezing," he whispered. "It must run along the outer wall."

We continued until we came to another ladder. Thomas sheathed his sword and began to climb. This was slightly harder for me as the opening was too wide to brace back against, and I would have to try to balance myself as I moved my hand up to the next rung. I paused once and held on, pulling myself close to the ladder.

I heard laughter, and muffled voices. "Thomas," I whispered. "Wait." I moved my head to the side of rungs and pressed my ear against the stones. The voices came in a little louder, but still too blurred together to distinguish.

"It helps if you have a cup," came a bitter voice from above us.

I yelped, dropped the lantern, and when it shattered below we were plunged into darkness. I heard a heavy sigh echo through the tunnels as though the castle itself was disappointed with me.

"Amazing that you two are the Laborers," came the voice again. It sounded much like Piter, but it was difficult to tell in the echoes. I heard shuffling, a faint ring that I thought was Thomas' sword coming free again. There was a rasp, and a faint globe of light marked the edges of the ladder above us. "You'll find it hard to climb with that in your hand, Thomas. And if you drop it, another light—which, I assume, you value highly—could very accidentally be shattered." The sentence cut off strangely just at the end, kind of clipped like shears swiftly pruning. "Come up, please."

The light moved a little way off, and Thomas began again to climb. I came slowly behind him, heart still hammering. When I finally came to the top, Thomas gripped my arm to steady me as I moved onto the platform that the Fool's light now showed. I also saw several other tunnels—these would need to be crawled through—branching away.

Piter sat forlorn on his stool, chin in his hand as he stared at the lantern. "I see you found me. I was beginning to fear you would take too long, and I would starve." He nudged a sack at his feet and one wrinkled apple rolled slowly from the mouth.

There were no other chairs, so I knelt on the floor where I could still see Piter's eyes. Thomas remained standing, hand on his sword hilt though he did not grip it.

"We thought you had run away—fled the castle."

He picked at his lip. "No. I needed to be found. The *truth* needs to be found. It has hidden with fools for too long."

"Why not just come forward? I thought his Lordship trusted you."

Piter frowned, and his lip trembled. "He did," he whispered, then cleared his throat. "He shouldn't have, but he did. Now look where we are." He glanced around the dim landing, a strange smile quirking his lips.

"So you set up the clues?" I asked. He nodded. "Why?"

"I knew you would figure it out."

"But, why us?" I asked.

Piter's eyes flashed to mine. "'Judge not, condemn not,' I believe you said. I needed someone who would listen. Actually listen. Someone who hadn't been there the first time, who could see the facts as facts, not as part of some complex story. Someone—" He twirled his hands as he tried to conjure the word. "Someone who was not close to Mistress Pendrel."

"Did you kill her?" Thomas asked.

Piter glared at him as he straightened. "No," he said. But then his gaze wavered, sought my face as he sagged again. "And yes."

I held up a hand to stay Thomas. "Explain yourself," I said quickly.

"I was a good court jester," he said, his voice low. "I fell into it—my father had not been, nor his father. But I could caper, and I was fearless, and I caught his Lordship's eye once while he was making his way through town. I mocked him then, at barely twelve years old, but he loved it. And I only grew better. Sometimes"—his gaze pierced me again—"I could look into someone and see exactly how to lance them, without ever meeting them before."

"Yes, we noticed," I said with a grin and a glance at Thomas.

"Yes. Although you were something else entirely." He shook himself. "Anyway. I was very good. Mistress Pendrel, she would have been good too. She would have made a terrible lady—terrible. And I tried to warn them."

"Favish noticed she would not sit still at the table."

"Favish!" Piter fumed. "That oafsome meddler. Are you going to take his side?"

"You left the note out for us to find."

Piter grumbled incoherently. "Well, you weren't supposed to actually read them. Anyway, that dinner was before I started…" His lip trembled again and he paused to master it. "Before I started teaching her."

My eyebrows shot up. "You taught her to be a court jester?"

He glowered. "Judge...not," he snarled. He sighed and looked away. "And no, not the way you put it. I taught her to caper and tumble. She was restless, and pestered me about it. And she would positively light up when I performed, and I could see her mimicking the movements—discreetly, though, just motions with her hands. But when she performed the full motions, she was *good.* She had near surpassed me."

"I don't see how this meant you killed her but didn't..." I trailed off as I began to perhaps see what had happened. Judge not, he had said, though.

"The one thing she lacked was discretion," he continued. "She was prone to getting caught, and raising storms among the Lord and Ladyship. They knew I continued to teach her, and began threatening me." He sank lower again, his gaze fast on the flame. "I begged her to stop—I knew she would never stop practicing, and no one with such skill should be made to. But if she could please stop getting caught." He paused again to sigh deeply. "So, she found remote places to practice, and eventually realized the roof of the tower was as secluded as she could get. No one outside would see her, and her Ladyship only went up there to watch for Lord Pendrel's coming if he was away, or when the weather was fairest."

"And she could have you give warning if someone was coming up unexpectedly from below. Or, direct them another way if they were looking for her."

He nodded bitterly. "It had been days since she had gotten the opportunity, and she chafed for it. I knew his Lordship was actually at home because of my secret ways, and her Ladyship was occupied. So I sent Penelope away. When I tried to go aloft, that nursemaid Lanette came by and I had to retreat. By the time I made my way to the top, Joliette was gone. I thought she had returned to her chambers or somewhere. It was drawing late in the day. So, I left." His eyes were steady on mine. "I left," he repeated, softer this time.

It was silent on the landing. In Piter's eyes I saw him reliving that day. I could almost imagine it myself—so many simple choices, strung together to such a catastrophic end. Perhaps I saw it so easily because I had a few of those simple choices of my own. Enough to know that simply saying "it's not your fault" would carry no weight. Or, the weight it carried would be even more guilt, since placing fault was the obvious conclusion. By acknowledging it, even negatively, I would reinforce it.

"How was Lady Pendrel occupied?" I asked instead. "You said you knew she was."

"Yes. Well. Perhaps her Ladyship can fill you in on that detail." He shrugged. "That's not my story to tell."

"So, Lord Pendrel made a show of returning, conducted the investigation, and found no guilt. It was an accident." I said the last firmly, without trying to oversay it. Just enough, hopefully, to redraw the obvious conclusion.

"Of course," he said drily. "And I said nothing that might bring necessary implications to myself."

"Yes, well, that may have to change, Piter," I replied. "Before we drag you off to his Lordship, though: how did Favish end up dead in your clothes?"

"That had nothing to do with me, and everything to do with Favish," he spat. "He is the true fool—spent too much time in the archives wishing his stories were more exciting. He saw plot and conflict everywhere—a mouse left a cheese crumb, Favish thought it was someone trying to send messages or find their way home. Idiot." Piter drew a deep sigh. "Facts. He should have stuck to facts instead of being so caught up in 'the whole experience.'"

"He did give me something of a speech about it," I said.

"He gave it to everyone. So, despite the facts, he had to spin his story—give it context, characters, emotion..."

"What story did he spin about you?"

"There were two he favored. One, that Joliette and I were involved in some illicit and immoral affair." Piter shook his head, scrubbed his hands down his face. "Sometimes I wonder—well, no matter. The one more important to him was that I killed her. Shoved her off the tower for...reasons."

"What reasons?"

"You know, he never told me. Just that he was sure I did. Threatened to go to his Lordship about it years ago when it first happened."

"He didn't, though."

"Of course not! All I had to say was that I wasn't around when it happened, and Lord Pendrel believed me—with just cause," he said, waiting until I nodded to continue. "Favish, as I said, had no actual reasons and he knew it. So I thought it was over. Except the dragon, and eventually she started showing up again. Favish was convinced it was because I had escaped justice, that Joliette's ghost came back for me. Then you two come along, and Favish knew the situation would be investigated again. He thought he had another chance at me."

"Why do you think Joliette's ghost is showing up?" I asked.

Piter blew out his cheeks as he gazed off down one of the dark crawl spaces. "Someone hasn't let her go," he murmured. "We all mourn her passing, we all wish her back. Probably someone wants it more than others."

"Who?"

Piter shrugged, absorbed—it seemed to me—in wherever that

tunnel led.

I glanced at Thomas. When he looked at me, I felt my Fire flicker a question. I didn't understand where it might lead, but I asked it. "Why was Favish convinced you had more to do with Joliette's death? There had to be something else."

"He didn't like me anymore."

"'Anymore.' What happened?"

"I stole his key."

"Why did you do that?"

His eyes flicked to mine. "I'm a jester."

"Okay, yes, but why that?"

"My job is to dig at the root of who people think they are, do you understand that? For his Lordship, I make sure he remembers he is still a human being—he may be Lord of this Manor but he still uses a garderobe." Piter shrugged. "Favish *obsessed* over that key. Wore it around—not to keep it safe—but so everyone knew what he thought he was. That the history of castle Fosse somehow was under his control and dictation. *He* would decide if your actions warranted entry into the archives, and the light in which he cast you—facts aren't enough, are they? With the right—or wrong—embellishment, you would be forever remembered as either a light or an aberration on the life of this castle. And he did love to wield it. So I took it. Locked him out of his precious records. I hoped he would realize how unimportant they were, in the face of all human history."

"It didn't work."

Piter's eyes went wide as he shook his head. "Oh, no. Not at all. That pride was too deeply rooted by then. Instead of digging out the roots, I made them bitter."

I nodded. Not that I might have known better in his place, but I could recall some who had let their sense of self attach too fully to something. As soon as it was gone or threatened, they acted in the most terrifying of ways. Judith, for one, thought far too much of her piety.

"So, Favish couldn't put the blame on you back then. But he's trying again now?"

"He thought you two would figure it out, if anyone would. He told me he was close to coming right to you with it, if I didn't speak up."

"Why didn't he? Why do it this way?" I asked. Piter only shrugged. "You also haven't explained how he got hold of your clothes."

"Ah. Well. Seems I wasn't the only one able to steal keys. And I did warn you when I first took you to meet him."

I goggled. "How long has he had them?"

"I wasn't sure he did, when I said it. But they had gone suspiciously missing shortly after I was made to return his key and apologize. I suppose he thought my pride was wrapped in them just as his is wrapped in his particular office."

"It isn't though," I said.

He smiled. "I'm a fool without or without clothes."

I shook my head, looked at Thomas. "Something still isn't right. I believe your story, as far as you know it, as far as you're telling it. But there must be more."

"The murderer I thought I heard," Thomas murmured.

"Yes, exactly." I turned back to Piter. "Amaury. Journeyman mason. Do you know him?"

"There was one I never had to jest," Piter said. "Never thought too highly of himself, or strove for...well, anything, really. I think he only made Journeyman from one of Favish's embellishments."

"How so?"

"Oh, his wonderful contexts. Made it seem like a wall Amaury had built saved Penelope from certain death, and only because he had made sure it was constructed so well. Maybe even saved Mistress Pendrel as well—though she was so far away from the scaffolding when it collapsed she probably would not have even heard it hit the ground except Penelope screamed."

"Why did Favish do that, write the embellishment?"

"Well," Piter said in a conspiratorial whisper. "From the talk of the servants, it just might be that Amaury and Favish were related, in some sordid way. Maybe even..." He glanced side to side at the empty crawl spaces. "Brothers."

I looked at Thomas, saw in his eyes the same recognition I felt. "Funny thing, family," I said. "We don't choose them, and sometimes we do the most awful things to protect them." I looked at Piter again, who seemed confused. "Even trying to pin their blame on someone else, who we don't particularly like anyway."

Chapter 13

Thomas and I strode down the hall, the Fool following dutifully behind us. So much of what he had said swirled in my thoughts, but behind it all was still the question of the dragon and what part it played in all this. And yet, a small voice of peace assured me we were doing what was necessary.

Which also helped, since we were on our way to bring difficult truths to his Lordship. And hard questions.

I had thought to find Joliff first, but he moved around so much in his duties I quickly thought better of it. So instead we headed straight for the master chambers. I knocked lightly. "Lordship? It's Rae-Anna and Thomas, sir."

After a moment the door opened, and when his eyes moved beyond us they widened. "Thome! Where were you? Boris will be beside himself, you must apologize to him. And to me!"

"Lordship," I interjected. "There is much we must speak with you and her Ladyship about. May we meet somewhere private?"

"Of course, come inside," he said. He took a step back, and waved us in when we hesitated. "No, do. I promise all will be well."

With a quick glance at Thomas I went inside, and they all fell in behind me—Piter perhaps with more confidence. He knew the Pendrels better, after all.

When I was fully inside, it was my turn to goggle. Seated smugly in a corner was Favish, arms crossed as he watched Piter turn white as the curtains adorning the master bed. Lady Pendrel was seated nearby, hands folded demurely in her lap, but with a patient look on her face.

Piter looked as though he wanted to leave, which—I assumed—was why Boris came up behind him to stand in the way of his escape.

"Now your day will come," Favish said. Lord Pendrel quickly raised a hand to forestall him.

"Antagonizing him will accomplish nothing," he said. He turned to Thomas and I. "Well then. We're all here. Tell us the story, please."

I hesitated, surprised by Favish's smug assurance. When Piter was speaking in his loft I felt sure of all the pieces I had assembled, but now...

Be not afraid...

"But speak," I muttered to myself. "If I may, Lordship," I continued aloud. "I would be interested in Favish's story—and yours, it seems—that brings him back from the dead."

"Quite simple," Favish leered, but Lord Pendrel held up a hand again.

"Forgive me, Favish, but I do fear for your emotions in this case. The story is this: Favish thought, with two laborers for the Beloved searching out the truth, it might be time for Joliette's murderer to finally come to light. It was his idea—brilliant, too—to enact this double-deceit to bring suspicion on Piter as a murderer. So we built an effigy, dressed it in Piter's foolscap, and tossed it off the tower. When the 'body' was found, and suddenly Favish missing, we knew you two would seek out Piter and perhaps extract a confession."

I frowned. "Clever," I admitted. "We would have the chance to speak to nearly everyone in the castle under suspicion of murder, and redo your investigation for you. While saving her Ladyship from the stress of it, too. Very clever." I glanced at Thomas with a nod, taking stock of Piter as well. He seemed to have recovered a little, but there was a dangerous light in his eye. "Thomas," I murmured, directing his attention to Piter. He glanced back, saw it as well, and positioned himself to intercept the Fool if he needed to. I turned my attention back to Favish and Lord Pendrel, who regarded me curiously.

"What is it, lady?" he asked.

"Favish, do you believe in The Beloved?" I asked.

He grinned crookedly. "Of course I do," he said, though he hesitated.

"And do you fear Our Father?"

He swallowed. "All my life."

"Once more, if it pleases you: do you believe in the power of His Sacred Fire?"

"Rae-Anna, what is this?" Lord Pendrel asked.

"I do—everything you say, yes, I do," Favish said hurriedly.

I cocked my head. "Favish, you do not."

"Mistress Rae-Anna, I demand you explain yourself," Lord Pendrel said. "What did Piter say to you?"

"Lord Pendrel, forgive me," I said, inclining my head. "But it seems to me that any double-deceit Favish thought to conjure would be less important than knowledge provided by Our Father Himself."

"What knowledge?" Lord Pendrel asked.

"Who is Amaury?"

"I told you, a Journeyman mason—"

"My brother," Favish said quietly. The smugness was gone, now. "I think I see the beginnings of a true and holy fear in your eyes, Favish," I said gently. "Do you want to tell the story?"

Whatever it was I saw, though, winked out instantly and was replaced by a hardened and bitter root. He clamped his mouth shut and shook his head. As I stood in silence, praying for his heart to soften, he spat: "You can't prove anything."

Both Pendrels were now fixated on me. Lady Pendrel's gaze held a pleading note to it. "Forgive me if you think I am being insensitive," I said. "Mercy and Patience are closely bonded, and Our Father extends both in generous quantities. I try to do the same." I paused again, but Favish folded his arms. "Where Favish went wrong was to think that by deceit alone he might obtain a truth that suited him. The Sacred Fire needs no duplicity. You knew, Lordship, that Thomas heard the whisperings of Joliette's murderer. And that, as we spoke to everyone from the Hall, that Amaury was known to him. Not Piter, Lordship."

"Yes, but he wasn't sure—and he had not spoken to Piter at that time."

"But I had before, Lordship," Thomas murmured. "The voice was none I had heard before that night."

Lord Pendrel looked at Favish, who looked away. "Go on," he said, his voice—not defeated, but the voice of one who knew his assurances had been false.

"It is true, Lordship, that Piter knew Joliette was on the tower top—knew why, and directed Penelope away, so that Joliette would be free to practice what she loved. What he did not know, my lord, was that someone went up to the tower after he had dodged away from Lanette."

"Amaury," Lord Pendrel breathed.

"Yes, my lord."

"Why?"

I again looked at Favish, but though his eyes were open it felt as though he was ignoring all that was being said. "Sometimes, my lord, a guilty conscience will see in others what we do not wish to see in ourselves—or in those closest to us."

"He was assailing her!" Piter cried out. "And you tried to accuse me of it!"

Thomas reached out and grabbed Piter as he tried to rush by. Lord Pendrel seemed too stunned to move. But Lady Pendrel bolted to her feet as her hand cracked against Favish's face. As she screamed incoherently, hands still flailing, Lord Pendrel came to himself and pulled her away.

"Amaury said she had fallen!" Favish shouted, his arms cradling his head though the blows had ceased. "He had not touched her, but as she fled she fell. An accident!" His eyes burned at the Pendrels. "And where were you? You cared so little, you sent her off every chance you could. It's just as much your fault!"

Lady Pendrel cried aloud, but his Lordship was in a fury. "Boris!" he shouted. The Captain came forward and dragged Favish roughly away, who did little to defend himself. Perhaps, finally, he knew justice had come to him.

When Favish was finally gone from the chambers, Piter calmed first, though his chest still heaved. Lady Pendrel's wails quieted to a low murmur. Lord Pendrel looked to us. "Was it an accident?"

Thomas shook his head. "Not from the whispers I heard, my lord. She threatened Amaury on that tower. Afraid he would be found out, he pushed her. I also think the 'accident' of the fallen scaffolding was arranged by him, somehow, to seem to be her hero. He hoped, out of gratitude, she would warm to him and also put him in your good graces."

Lord Pendrel shook his head sadly. "I never knew him to be so conniving," he murmured.

I hesitated. "My lord, despite Favish's claim of ignorance, he seems to me to be the cleverer. It could be he helped Amaury in that, too."

Lord Pendrel looked to Piter. "Please accept my humble apologies, Piter," he said. "I had trusted you before, and should have kept doing so. I am sorry as well for the discomfort of the past day."

Piter straightened his tunic. "Of course, my lord, we are all fools in our turn." A faint mischievous sparkle came to his eye, and Lord Pendrel waggled a finger at him.

"Do you think the dragon will be gone? Was that injustice why it was here?"

I sought the Fire. It still burned brightly. I shook my head slowly. "I do not, my Lord. And there remains some unanswered questions. Why was Mistress' ghost appearing? Someone had to be calling her up—"

"It was me," Lady Pendrel murmured. She glanced up at her husband, who managed to soften the shocked look on his face. "I didn't realize I was doing it, at first—that is, I knew someone from my father's demesne who claimed she could do it. She said she had given me the power, but I did not think it was working. It was only delayed at first. The more I did it, the faster she would come."

"That's why you came to the tower when I was there," I said with a nod. Again I felt a question rising from the Fire, though I did not want to ask it. "My Lord, my Lady: Thomas and I asked Piter, who seemed to know, but he said it was not his story. Favish asked it as well."

"Where were we?" Lord Pendrel said softly. I nodded, and they looked at each other. Lady Pendrel's face pinked, and she turned her face against his chest. Lord Pendrel cleared his throat. "We were together," he said. I looked at Piter, who was looking discreetly away, and at Thomas, who tried to avoid my eyes. My gaze returned as it dawned on me.

"You needed an heir," I said simply. His lordship nodded once, though I still saw guilt written on his face. He would not have to sneak back to the castle if it was for duty only. "And that's..." *That's why you have not produced one since. You feel too guilty to try.* "I'm sorry, my Lord. And my Lady. I cannot imagine... I'm sorry."

I turned and left the room. I did not stop for two turns down the hallway. Finally I leaned a hand against the stone, trying to calm myself. After a few moments I heard footsteps behind me and turned to see Thomas approaching slowly.

"Are you okay?" he asked.

"I've been an idiot—again," I said.

His brow furrowed. "You?" he asked. I cocked an eyebrow, but he had asked honestly. "I mean, in what way. Which part of this series of events... It seems like you put together far more than me—"

I waved him off. "I know what you mean. No, I've been unfair to you. For my part, I don't really blame you—I promise, I don't. But I didn't make it easy on you, or actually try to help you."

"And for my part, I don't know how to help me either," he said.

"Which still doesn't make you at fault." I closed my eyes and sighed. "I think part of me wants just one thing to be normal for us. Is that wrong? Is it so bad to say: 'in all these other things, do as You will; but give us one thing that is not, I don't know, shocking, horrible, terrifying, strange, unpredictable—"

He came to me and held me as I vented a frustrated sigh. "What is normal?" he asked.

I shrugged. "I guess that's true," I admitted. "But I hoped we could be a normal husband and wife, at least in some regards. Even if we aren't living the normal life of a serf while we we're doing it."

Thomas drew a slow breath. "I've been wondering about that, too," he said. "And wondering—is it about us, though? I mean, what role will we play in Our Father's Kingdom? What parable is he telling through our obedience? Right?"

I shrugged again. "I suppose so. No, you're right. Ours, at least, is not a story of normal people living normal lives in obedience to Our Father's calling. I knew I was rejecting that even in Holden. I do envy them a little, those who are called to quiet lives."

"Of course—and I do too, sometimes. But Judith kind of made that choice for me. No matter who I married, I would probably have to deal with this. And my spouse as well. I'm sorry, in a way, that it's you..."

I shook my head. "No, because we're not normal, right?" I gave him a crooked smile. "It would be far worse for a farmwife. She would be expecting children, and a lot of them, and all her friends and family would be expecting that as well. At least for us, it would make our journey far more difficult if I was with child."

He went quiet, pulled me closer and rested his chin on my head. "Is that something you want?" he murmured.

I turned my head against his chest. "Maybe one day. If we ever get to live a normal life." I smiled, though he wouldn't be able to see it. "Like I said, it would complicate things even more if it happened now."

"Our Father can probably keep it that way, if it's His will, even if we...live like a normal husband and wife."

"Ah, but we shouldn't test Him either. Maybe He would use it to teach us to rely on Him even through tremendous hardship. Either way, I realized I carried unfair expectations, and I'm sorry."

"What made you realize?"

"The Pendrels," I said. "To be doing that when their daughter dies—is murdered because someone else wanted her for their depraved ends... *And they that are The Beloved's have crucified the flesh with the affections and lusts.* It's a terrible motivator, and a hollow way to spend one's energy, in such pursuits. Fine in its place, but to be sick with longing for it?" I shook my head, then twisted to gaze up at him. "And how much more so when you have such a wound concerning that thing. Instead of caring for you and seeking your healing, I was selfishly demanding what, as you said, has no real import in Our Father's Kingdom—not given His call on our lives right now."

Thomas nodded. "I appreciate that," he said. "It's not fair to you either, who did nothing to cause it. I am working on it." He sighed and shook his head. "I didn't think about it that way, but you're right. About the Pendrels, I mean this time. To live with that burden, to be chasing something so meaningless as lust when your only child was killed."

"Yes. But not strange to this story, is it? Everyone here that we've talked to had made some choice, it seemed so innocent and normal in the moment—justified, often times—but had the most disastrous consequences."

The castle seemed to shudder as a great boom echoed from somewhere above. The lanterns along the walls flickered, as though a wave of darkness rolled through. But my Fire rose strong and indignant, and I could feel Thomas' Seed grow thick roots as it sprouted.

"Even we questioned some of our own choices, didn't we," he said. Our gazes met and locked. "And worried and fretted over one moment in time."

Another rending crash echoed, another wave of darkness—this one more palpable—rolled through. Yet we, like old rocks in the pounding surf, remained fast.

"Almost as though we were stuck," I continued. "Never able to leave, never sure of the passing of time. One error, that felt fatal—and perhaps it was, to our minds and our spiritual growth."

A shriek accompanied the thundering echo this time, and the torches went out in the blast of darkness. Behind it was a many-hued light, shimmering along the walls, as though it sought us out.

I only caught it in my periphery though, as I continued to gaze into Thomas' eyes.

"I love you, Thomas," I said. "And with The Beloved guiding and strengthening our efforts, we will both be healed, and both move forward in this abnormal life to which He called us."

He smiled, his eyes tracing every line and scar on my face. "Rae-Anna," he whispered. "I see your face—yours only. I know you, and love you."

The shimmering lights faded as the corridor went silent. I felt Thomas' lips on mine, and I tangled my fingers in his hair as I held him. We parted as we heard the door down the hall screech open. Lord Pendrel appeared, eyes goggling.

"What is happening?" he asked.

"The dragon is attacking," I said. "Gather everyone in the hall."

Chapter 14

They came in twos and threes, and sometimes batches, as the servants herded them. It was not meal time, so most came obediently but obviously confused. The tables had not been set out yet, so they milled and conversed, adding a general din to the hall. From conversations held by those nearest to us, I could tell many assumed it was about the murder.

"My lord, you may need to explain Favish's duplicity first," I said. "It will be easier for them to listen if that mystery is put to rest."

He nodded, and when Joliff came to report all citizens had been gathered he raised his hands. The silence scattered and spread until all eyes were fixed on him, with one or two sideways glances at Thomas and I.

"Before I give Rae-Anna leave to speak," he said, and a few more glances shifted my way. "I want to first say the murder of young Mistress Pendrel has been solved." There was another general clamor at this, and Lord Pendrel had to wave his arms to restore silence. "I know. All evidence we could gather at the time pointed to an accident. However, through the power of the Sacred Fire given to her, Rae-Anna—and Thomas—were able to piece together more than I. It is a terrible tale, perhaps fit for another time to be told in full, but confessions have been made and evidences collected. The murderer is no more, and those who had covered it up have met justice.

"And now, Rae-Anna has asked us all to gather in regards to the dragon of Fosse." He gestured to me, and stepped aside. As one, all eyes shifted to me and fixed.

I realized then I was much better at face to face conversations. I swallowed once, twice. Thomas touched my arm gently. "Seek the Fire," he whispered.

For the Holy Ghost shall teach you in the same hour what ye ought to say.

"Through no fault of His Lordship," I began, willing the Fire into my voice. It came out far stronger than I anticipated. "He, and many of you, are trapped here." I expected the outcry that arose, waited a moment for it to build, then raised my hand for silence. "I say that only to impress on you how serious the situation is."

"How are we trapped? Is it the guards?"

"And who is trapped? Can *you* leave?"

I let a piece of a smile curve my lips. "I believe I am trapped too, but trapped so that I may help you find freedom," I replied to the second question. "As to the first question: it is the dragon. Or rather, what the dragon represents." I looked around the room. "Your regrets."

Thunder rumbled, and I knew the dragon had come—assumed he probably would. He would not let them leave without a fight. More than one gaze broke from mine to look up at the vault above, or to the windows. I felt it before I saw again the darkness, now leaking in the windows like smoke. It struck the floor and spread.

"For Thomas and myself, we have suffered injury by another. We were attacked in a moment of weakness, taken advantage of by those we should have been able to trust. Those wounds have not yet healed, and the scars are often difficult to take account for. We each could think of one decision, one moment in time that if we had chosen differently, had turned left instead of right, then perhaps those hurts would have been spared us."

The smoke thickened, began sending tendrils like vines around people's ankles. Those ensnared were able to keep their eyes on me, but I could sense a struggle going on inside as they battled perhaps fear, perhaps their own memories of pain—I could not tell.

"But no matter the pain, Our Father can heal us, and redeem those exact hurts. The thing that we think has ruined our lives, if we give it to Our Father for wisdom and guidance, can be exactly that which propels us into the life and work He planned in advance for us to do."

The tendrils thickened, and a few tightened. I heard a low moan come from several throats—not as though the tendrils hurt, but I wondered if it was remembered pain, or the dragon exerting his will.

"So your god did this to us?" a voice called out, rasping and low. Contemptuous. And it sounded like Mahmoud. "To make us need him?"

"No," I said firmly. "Each of us chooses what we will do, and those actions bring either joy or pain. If we choose according to the will of Our Father, we will spread justice, joy, blessings, and peace. If we choose according to our will, we risk bringing that pain, injustice, suffering, and conflict. It may not—that is part of Our Father's general blessings on us, that we can find some semblance of joy without Him. But no choice made according to His specific plan and with His Sacred Fire will do ultimate harm to ourselves or anyone around us."

Thunder crashed again, directly above, and a few bits of stone rained down into the hall. There was a roaring, this time I knew because of the truth being spoken over these captives of his. Freedom was nearer.

I turned quickly to Lord Pendrel. "My lord, you and the Lady Pendrel each have moments in time that you regret above all others. And I perceive, my Lord, that you have relived those moments over and over, and continue to define your life in terms of the catastrophe those choices enabled. Relived them so much that Thomas and I, when listening to them, thought they were quite recent. But the death of Mistress Pendrel was—how many years ago?"

He paused to consider, distracted now and again as the dragon beat himself against the roof, trying to breach it. Thick darkness flooded through the windows now, filling the hall to people's waists. He squinted his eyes shut, then shouted, "eight years! It was nearly over eight years ago."

I heard a few gasps and murmurs from the room. Others, it seemed, had also forgotten. "Eight years," I repeated. "You have stayed in that moment, in your thoughts, have you not?"

"We cannot just move on," he said desperately.

"My Lord, I do not ask you to forget her, to simply 'move on' as though nothing had happened. But neither can you undo it. You cannot change that day, cannot change the choices you made. But if you want to be free, you will need to begin choosing according to the needs of today, not the wishes of yesterday."

I turned to the hall as the darkness crept to people's chins. "Each of you must remember whatever day, whatever event, has you trapped and recognize that those moments, those choices cannot be changed. To be free, you must choose this day according to this day's needs, according to tomorrow's needs. To find for yourself again a future that you can move *toward*, not just a past you wish to run away from."

A roar blasted into the hall, and with tucked wings the dragon slipped through a narrow window. He soared overhead, a little smaller than I remembered him, though the darkness boiling from his mouth belied his size. Multi-hued eyes cast around the room, fixing each person before moving on. I felt his gaze sweep across me, though for now his attention stayed on the inhabitants of castle Fosse.

Thomas left my side, whispering something quickly to Lord Pendrel. They both moved off, and Thomas gestured quickly for me to keep talking.

"For others, perhaps you had to leave something behind—something you knew was damaging. And yet it had brought some comforts. Since moving on, you see only the hardships facing you now and only the good parts of what you left behind. Like the ancient Hebrews, you wish you could return to your slavery. For there, at least, you had food and water along with your burdensome and hard labor. Our Father's arm is not so short! Even now he has prepared for you this day your daily bread. He has promised—and so perhaps what looks like too little is actually just enough."

Another roar from overhead, and again I thought the dragon seemed smaller. Large as the hall was, I knew he would have filled it before. Now he seemed more like an oversized bird.

Despite his size his gaze was still terrible, the fear and darkness he spread no less diminished. The hall was nearly filled, and I could only see over it because of the dais on which I stood.

The people which sat in darkness saw great light; and to them which sat in the region and shadow of death light is sprung up.

I strode down from the dais, let the swirling darkness envelop me. The Fire sprang up inside, pushed the darkness just far enough back that by reaching out I could only touch it with my fingertips. Beyond that I could see nothing. But I knew there had been people there, people who could not move and might not bear the Fire the way I did.

But the clouds must have confused distance as well as sound and sight, because where I thought to find a throng I still only found an individual here, one there. As the light around me reached them, their eyes would be screwed tight. They were covered as though with a fine plaster, barely breathing. I would touch them, speak a word of encouragement from the Holy Words as the Fire gave me utterance. Often times the dust would fall away and their eyes would open wide as they gulped air. I would point them toward the dais—I could see the ceiling above me, and could still orient myself that way—and they would move off in their own safe pocket.

Other times when I spoke encouragement the plaster grew thicker, their breathing shallower, and I feared they died. I would pause to pray earnestly when I could, but always I felt the insistence that I move deeper through the crowd. There were so many trapped, so many living in fear or doubt or hopelessness—some may die while I tended those who were beyond reaching. And so I would leave, watch the swirling darkness cover them again. More than once I thought I felt a spirit cry out as though being squeezed, choked of its life as regret and loss buried it. So often I almost turned back, nearly weeping, but I could not resist the pull. Soon I would find another, the Words this time set them free, and for a moment I would be relieved again.

But the further I went, the more those I had to leave behind weighed on me, dragging at my feet as though I carried their bodies with me. The Fire was pitiless as it made me stagger on and on. *Can you not lead me only to those who will be saved?* I pleaded. I could not take leaving another soul to the clutches of the darkness.

The Lord is not slack concerning his promise, as some men count slackness; but is not willing that any should perish, but that all should come to repentance.

But surely you already know who will be saved or not! Father, I cannot take any more.

All day long I have stretched forth my hands unto a disobedient and gainsaying people. How then shall they call on him in whom they have not believed? And how shall they believe in him of whom they have not heard? And how shall they hear without a preacher?

I groaned, but leaned myself on the Fire and pressed on. Person after person, all isolated and trapped, some responding, some not. Once I glanced up as a roar echoed faintly down into my small space, saw the dragon most assuredly even smaller now. *The more people I free, the smaller he becomes. Surely soon he will be able to be defeated!*

I continued in that knowledge with renewed vigor. If I could just reach five or ten more, I thought. Surely the darkness coming from the dragon would lessen, or weaken. Or the Fire would suddenly banish it, freeing them all and dismissing the dragon from this realm! If only I could get to a few more. Just a few more...

I halted, standing before a small child. Trembling, desperately hopeful, I reached out in comfort. But my words died in my throat as the plaster thickened at my words.

"You cannot do this," I said. "She's a child! Surely she cannot be so enslaved by regrets at her age!"

I felt a slight tugging, pulling me onward. But I planted my feet. "No!" I shouted. "Not until you explain this to me!"

The Fire flickered, dimmed, and the darkness slammed a little closer to me, though it did not enshroud me yet. I grit my teeth, placed both hands on the girl's shoulders as I spoke every passage of hope I could remember. I did not see it soften, but neither did I see it harden. She looked vaguely familiar—difficult to tell under the plaster—and I tried to place her in the castle. There had been so many, though...

I heard a rattling hiss like laughter and I took an involuntary step backward as the dragon, now no larger than a lizard, rose up behind the girl's head. His tongue flickered as his lips curled into a smile. Though small, his shimmering eyes shone with all of their former intensity.

"You, get away," I seethed.

He shook his head as he clicked his tongue. "You don't have that power, little one. You can talk all you want, but this is not your choice."

I gave him a cruel smile. "Others have said the same before I banished them back to Abaddon."

He gave me a flat stare. "I am not from Abaddon," he said. "Men of free will give birth to me, and only by their free will can I go away."

I faltered a moment. I believed him, because it made sense. I hardened my resolve, forced power into my voice I wasn't sure I held. "You cannot take this one," I said. "She is not yours."

He climbed atop her head. "'Take' her? They are born mine. It is you who must try to take them from me."

I shook my head. "No. They belong to Him—to Our Father..."

He laughed again, the same chortling hiss. "No, little one. Because of the sin of First Man, all men are born mine." He scooted down onto her shoulder and looked into her face. "Tell me, have you ever seen a more selfish person than a child? Deny them the smallest thing, take away something that isn't even theirs, and they would move heaven and earth to take it back. Threaten to let someone else have what they have not even touched or thought about, and they will fight to repossess it."

"They are children, they don't know any better!"

"Exactly!" His shimmering eyes bored into mine. "They do not know any better, and act on their natural desires. They have to be trained, do they not? They must be taught. And there are many, young one, who do not care to teach any longer." He turned and gazed at the young girl again. "What is the most evil man but one who has grown up to be able to act on their most childish desires—now suddenly with greater power and effect? Take her?" he repeated, as his gaze swiveled to me. "All I have to do is keep you from her for just long enough to taste that power, the heady joy of self-absorption, the comfort and security of self-willed possession. And if they stray too far from me, I remind them of something they lost and cannot regain—and they will be so desirous to regain it they can go nowhere else."

"There's always a chance," I whispered.

He shrugged. "Chances work both ways," he sneered. "For every chance you get, I have five hundred to call on. You have to be present to offer that chance; my chances come in the deepest solitude, in the darkest dreams. No, young one, this one is mine and will stay that way."

"Not if I have any say."

He waggled a talon. "Speaking of you, I have asked for a chance at you—"

"You can't have it."

"Ah! Let me finish. I asked for a chance, and have been graciously allowed it."

"You'll find nothing," I said with as much force as I could muster. But I knew it was hollow—and, it seemed, so did he.

"You've gotten off easy," he said with a smirk. "You have been so focused on Thomas—what a sweet boy he was! His fields of regret were bursting with grain and new wine—"

"He's not yours either!"

"Sadly, you are right. I digressed. You, as I said, got off easy, and for far too long. Let's take a look at what you regret, shall we?"

I backed away again, but bumped into the darkness as a shifting but solid thing. "No," I said weakly.

The dragon sighed, but grinned malevolently. "The nice thing about making me so small is that I can invade you *so* much more easily."

He squatted, then launched himself at me. I put my hands up too late as he shot between them, striking me in the nose. I gagged as I felt him worm his way into my skull as the darkness closed in around me.

Chapter 15

Laughter faded as light came, sparkling at first, then turning white. I opened my eyes to blue skies between rooftops. My head throbbed a few times, but that quickly faded as I blinked.

"Thomas?" I muttered.

Faintly I heard the noise of streets—a clattering cart, clopping hooves, a hawker's cry, children calling out to one another. I sat up and looked around.

Holden.

I looked down, saw tattered and dirty clothes that I was all too familiar with. I swallowed. *Please, no.*

Do you remember what day this is?

I waited for something to come to mind. There had been too many days in Holden that had begun this way. While I thought, freezing water suddenly doused me.

"Off with ye!" a man shouted. "Ye'll not be begging at my door, Liar's child!"

I turned, recognizing the blacksmith. "I'm sorry," I heard myself mumble. I was not in control of my body, and I staggered to my feet and lurched down the lane away from his angry bellows.

Every where I went I saw familiarity and cold stares. Most in Holden had heard of me after the spectacle my mother and father had made of me. Most knew to turn me out. I couldn't even remember how I had ended up near Byron's. But in the cold and dark, many roads looked the same.

I turned a corner and bumped into someone. "Ooh! Careful!" she said. I looked up into Genevieve's face. Inside, I wept; outside, and at the time of the memory—obviously—I had no idea who she was or what she would become. At that time, she was a strange, friendly face. Probably she was not supposed to be out alone, but I recognized the fire of her independence immediately. She looked me up and down, assessed my situation as quickly as I had assessed hers. "Come with me," she said, grabbing my hand. I recoiled out of reflex, but followed her out of curiosity.

All of this was happening in accordance with the memory, and while I had no control over my thoughts and actions within it, I still had the knowledge of the present, as I knew the dragon had taken me back. And so I fought against the memory, trying to stop seeing it, or to run away from it. Maybe if I had never known Genevieve, things might have turned out differently for her...

She took me to the bridge, underneath to where the stream—when it wasn't swollen with spring rains—trickled between stony banks. Tucked underneath she had made something of a camp. "Make yourself at home," she said. "I'll be right back."

She left, and I remained stuck. I glanced out from beneath that bridge, seeing as if for the first time the belltower of the convent. My heart stirred with curiosity: *would the Sisters take me in, despite my curse? Could they help me lift it?*

Soon Genevieve was back with two small loaves of bread, and all thoughts of the convent fled away. "Parents die?" she asked, handing one to me.

"May as well have," I muttered. But when I reached for the loaf, I did so with my left hand.

"Oh," she said with a cocked eyebrow.

I snatched the loaf before she could retract it, and promptly devoured it.

She watched me, amused, as she ate her loaf languidly. "Just so you know, I don't care." She paused to look me up and down again. "Just don't burn me alive or anything."

I forgot she had said that. I wonder if she ever heard...

Suddenly my mind was free, and I ran as fast as I could. I could look back and see Genevieve and I still talking. She had been so kind, so talkative, and so generous in those early days. I didn't want to relive it.

So I dashed through Holden, intending to head for the convent, hoping I could reach some of the early memories there. But suddenly the streets made no sense. Turns that should have taken me westward took me east, and instead of working my way out of town only struggled deeper into it.

Shimmering light blazed around me as I pelted into an open square that I swore was not in Holden. In it were dozens of children, playing various games as children will do. A few skipped on a small stone walk, others were in the grass. A few boys were attempting to climb a tree. All paused in their games when I skidded to a halt and turned to stare at me. The wind rustled the tree tops, and as the sunlight dappled the yard, their eyes shifted from green to brown to blue, and back.

I turned again and ran away. Almost immediately I bumped into

Genevieve. "Come with me," she said again, grabbing my hand as she pulled me along. I didn't recoil this time—we were fast friends by then—but let her pull me along through streets now in their proper order.

Though my mind reeled, I was aware enough to recognize where we were going. And the more our route pieced together in my mind, the more I dreaded it, knowing where we had gone that day.

We stopped at her lair under the bridge first, where she had—magically, in my mind—produced a brush. She dunked my head under the water, letting the flow of it rinse out my hair. Then she scrubbed me with a threadbare cloth, brushed my hair, and plaited it.

"What are you doing?" I kept asking her.

"Shush," is all she would say, with a mischievous little grin. I would glance every now and again at the convent's belltower and wonder. When Genevieve was satisfied she marched me off again, still mute and mischievous, until she halted exuberantly in front of the tailor's.

"You cannot be serious," I said.

She turned and pressed her finger against my lips. "And you cannot keep silent. Wait here." She turned and entered the shop. Someone hissed behind me, and I turned to see them holding up a warding sign as they passed, her child staring wide-eyed at me. A man went by the opposite way, turning his head away.

The door opened and the tailor came out. He sighed gustily and turned back. "Gennie," he said wearily, but she pushed him from behind.

"She's my friend, Mister Frankie, and she needs your help. I'll tell my father you didn't help her."

"And he'll probably thank me and paddle you!"

She put her fists on her hips. "You don't have to *touch* her, Francois, just make her a dress. Doesn't even have to be that good, but I'll tell my father if you make it poorly."

"Genevieve," I began, but she thrust her finger up in front of her mouth again.

Francois glanced around, saw a crowd starting to gather, and gestured me hurriedly inside. "Don't want her relieving herself on the streets, do you?" he bellowed. I glanced back in time before the door shut to see everyone scurrying on their way.

"I'm sorry," I mumbled.

He grunted something wordless, pointing toward the back of the shop. "Get in there, then, now that you're inside. Do you have something on underneath that? Good, take that off so I can at least have some idea of you before I make this. Won't take me long, I just need to alter it."

I obeyed with one sullen look at Genevieve for putting us all in that situation. As I slowly slid off the outer dress, I heard Francois grunt again. "What's that from?" he asked, pointing.

I glanced down at my shoulder. "A stone. They throw them sometimes."

"What about those?"

I knew without being able to see where he pointed. "Sometimes they drive me away with sticks, too."

"Who? Who's doing that? Your parents?"

I shook my head. "I don't see my parents anymore. Boys. Girls. Other people..."

"Are you stealing?"

I glanced at Genevieve. She had been feeding me lately. "Not for a while, now," I replied simply.

"Fine. Stand there. Here, hold this up." I held the dress, and he made a few quick marks. "Get that other dress back on. Sit over there." He turned to his table and began working while I sat where he bid. Genevieve sat beside me, legs swinging.

"Who's your father?" I whispered to her. "I thought your parents were dead."

"Might as well be," she whispered back. She giggled until Francois glared at her. "Papa's a councilman. Mother has guests over, and I'm too often underfoot, as she says. So I leave." She shrugged, then focused on me. "I take some food with me, so it isn't actually stealing. Just so you know."

True to his word, Francois was soon finished and we were herded out of his shop. "Come on!" Genevieve said, yanking me again down an alleyway. "Put it on, quick." She glanced up and down the alley, but I only stared at her. "Hurry up! There's no one around."

"I can't change in the middle of the street!" I squeaked.

Then, before I could stop her, she grabbed the hem of my dress and yanked it upward. I protested, but she wrestled it off and threw it triumphantly away. I scrambled into the new one.

It felt amazing, despite how angry and ashamed I felt. There still seemed no one around, but she couldn't have known that for sure. And yet the cloth was so soft and felt so clean and light. And it fit, I had to admit, far better than the previous one. As she grabbed my hand and yanked me again down the street, I couldn't help but notice it flowed around my ankles almost like a real dress.

"How did you pay for this?" I demanded.

She rolled her eyes. "I didn't pay for it, my papa did—it's one of my old ones. They won't even notice it's missing. Ooh! There he is!"

I looked up, still a little agape at the dress and her admission—and generosity—and didn't register at first who she was talking about.

"Hi, Rae-Anna," said a quiet voice.

I swallowed awkwardly. "Oh. Hi, Thomas."

"Is that a new dress? It looks nice."

Genevieve folded her arms and stared triumphantly at me. "Um. Yes. It is—well, new for me." I smiled giddily.

In that euphoria my mind broke free again, and I ran again. I knew—*knew*—where the dragon was leading me and I desperately didn't want to go.

But the streets bent to his will, it seemed, and I only wormed my way deeper and deeper into Holden. I somehow arrived at the same square, now populated with adults deep in conversation. One or two had books, a rarity. Most were in fancy dress and sipped at goblets. It didn't quite fit, not in Holden. Once again they turned as one body to stare at me, motionless except for one who spun a leaf from the tree idly in his hand. This time, too, there was a strange hunger in their gaze as though they wanted to devour me—whether mind, body, or spirit, I could not tell. And so I turned once more.

This time I made it to the bridge before I found Genevieve. And when I went underneath to her little camp I could not take my eyes off the convent.

"Are you even listening?" she demanded.

I turned. "I'm sorry," I said. "I'm trying. I'm a little distracted today."

"No kidding."

"I just—this isn't a game for me, Gennie. You can come and go, still get what you need when you need it. You have a home—when you go back, I'm still out here, still being chased away. But maybe with the Sisters—"

"I was trying to be your sister," she said quietly.

I sighed. "Not like that—I mean at the convent. They might take me in, maybe even find a way to get rid of my curse."

"I don't think you're cursed. I like you a lot, and you're still so kind and smart—"

"It's not the same," I huffed, turning away to look at the belltower again. "What kind of life will I ever have, cursed like this? No one will give me work, certainly no one will ever marry me—like you get to have," I added, glaring at her.

She seemed taken aback. "Right. Of course, how could I forget—as though I wasn't *just* talking about that."

"Well, whatever, you'll still have it. And what, are you and your husband going to keep visiting me under the bridge and dragging me places, forcing me on the people here who do not want me?"

A tear trembled in the corner of her eye. "I guess not," she said.

"I have to go, Genevieve," I said firmly. "I think they have to take me in, and then they can help me. Every time I see their belltower I think about it. I'm sorry, but it's what I have to do."

"Fine," she said. "Go, take care of yourself. I'm sure Lasell and I—"

The name hit me like a thunderclap. "Lasell?" I blurted. "Why are you marrying him?"

"Oh, you're paying attention now? I thought you were done. Because my papa is making me, Rae-Anna, because it's good for the council if I do. Remember?"

Some of what she had said when I was distracted trickled in. "But you can't! He's...Genevieve, you know him. You know I know him—"

"What am I supposed to do?"

I sighed abruptly, then looked at the belltower. "Come with me," I said.

"Rae-Anna..."

"No, come with me. It will have to be better—"

"Not for me! Not with my family—and not with who I am. And not if you leave! Rae-Anna, I couldn't stand up to papa if I knew you wouldn't be here to help me."

I stared at her. "You can't ask that of me," I whispered.

"It won't be forever, I promise," she said, grasping my hands—the way she always did when she was about to drag me off where I wasn't willing to go. I yanked my hands away.

"Gennie, stop it! I'm not your baby sister, and I'm not your mother. You can stand up to your papa—I've seen you stand up to so many others besides him. I know you can do it. But I need to do this, please!"

Her arms hung limp by her side. "Fine," she said, and I heard all hope leave her voice. "You're right. You need to do it. For yourself." And her eyes bored into mine, full of unshed tears.

I turned my mind and ran away, into the dragon-twisted streets. I didn't care. I couldn't face it again, knowing what Thomas said happened to her after I had gone. I didn't even try to make it to the convent, I simply ran.

I reached the square to see it full of standing corpses, wreathed in flame and moaning eternally. I fell to my knees, knowing they were all the people at Castle Fosse I hadn't reached, couldn't turn away from their pasts, save from whatever moment they lost hope. The tree, too, was gnarled and bent, leafless and crackling in the heat. I felt a claw on my shoulder, knew the dragon had come to claim me too.

Beloved, forgive me. I didn't know what I was doing. I was selfish, and failed. Restore me, that I might help as many as I can.

As I cried, I felt my mind shift without my efforts. Darkness slid away, the noise of the roaring fading away on its last echoes. I was clutching the little girl in the hall at Fosse, who I now knew was Genevieve, was crying into what would have been her hair. *I'm so sorry, Gennie. I'm so sorry. I don't know how it could have gone differently.*

Father, give me another chance. Let me return to Holden, let me see Gennie again. I beg you. Protect her.

I realized a hand was on my shoulder, glanced up to see Thomas, saw the knowledge in his eyes. He held his sword limply at his side. And I knew, too, that he had been the tree in the square, under assault by the dragon, helpless but to watch me struggle through my regret.

"Welcome back," he said, somehow forcing strength into his voice I knew he didn't have.

"I'm sorry, Thomas," I said. "I didn't—I couldn't—"

He shushed me gently, took me into his arms. His sword clattered to the ground as he let it go, and I saw beneath its point the shriveled body of an earthworm—all that was left of the once-mighty dragon.

Chapter 16

Dinner that night was a strange affair, perhaps more for Thomas and I than anyone else. We remembered the fight with the dragon. As we overheard more and more conversations, and as we traded pleasantries with the Pendrels, it became clear we were the only ones. They all remembered gathering in the hall at his Lordship's request, of being told of Joliette Pendrel's murder, and that I had addressed them. But that was all.

At least, it was all they remembered of that afternoon.

But as we listened more, and observed their general demeanor, it was also clear that—for many—they had a newfound joy, free from the hindrance of regret. Instead of endless recitations of offenses received, they spoke of opportunities for their futures. Instead of wagging their heads at the memory of past faults, they showed renewed eagerness for chances to do good.

Thomas and I traded many glances—some in wonder, some in confusion, some in brief memories of our own regrets that had not departed, but were maybe a little less of a thorn in our sides.

We were the lucky ones—or, perhaps, those graciously rewarded for our efforts in the fight. Some, and far too many for my joy to be complete, clearly still held on to those hurts, kept open the scars of those old wounds by constant picking. They seemed confused, too, as though they remembered far more of those who would commiserate than they found now beside them. More than once I would see someone's countenance darken as they retold their tale, only to be met with a shrug and an offer to move on, to look to tomorrow, to recognize the fallibility of all people and not take it too personally. And I could see in their frowns they thought their pain being made light of.

And, in more than one, I recognized in the flesh those I had only before seen in plaster, made harder by my attempts at encouragement and reminding of the Holy Words, of Our Father's promises and guarantee of hope. I would grimace and pray, however futile it may have felt, knowing no prayer is futile even if it is not fulfilled.

This meal also seemed to last far longer than any but the first we'd had. Few could stop talking long enough to eat, and the trays waiting to be set out began to pile up as the ones on the tables were still not emptied. And few minded. Finally, those still soured on their regrets departed—unsatisfied, I dare say, in stomach or grumbles—and the hall grew even louder.

Piter entered at some point, though his japes were hard to hear over the rest of the feasters. And, if any laughed, it was not unusual as most were laughing here and there. Lord and Lady Pendrel fairly glowed in their re-invigorated hall, and their joy, too, was not just for the residents of Castle Fosse but in each other.

Finally, the various fowl, beef, and pork was consumed, and most of the dainties. The pies were laid out, some cut, most still steaming. The jugs were running dry, though the cups were still full. And Lord

Pendrel rose, holding his aloft. Conversation ceased immediately, and everyone rose with mug aloft to meet his.

"Friends all," he began, and wide smiles broke out everywhere. "The lady and I are truly blessed tonight to have all of you with us—none more so than Rae-Anna and Thomas, who through the blessing and grace of Our Father finally brought justice to Joliette. To our daughter." He paused a moment to swallow and blink. "First, to Joliette. A light undimmed, forever remembered; she has found rest in the Kingdom on High, and eagerly awaits those who will join her in dancing upon those streets."

We all took a drink in a bittersweet joy. Lord Pendrel cleared his throat. "Second, to Rae-Anna and Thomas. Hopefully they may enjoy the rest of the winter here at Castle Fosse in more mundane pursuits. Though any time Rae-Anna wants to grace us with treaties on the Holy Words we would be most honored."

I curtsied shallowly before we all drank, and Thomas beamed at me. For which, of course, I gave him a short curtsy as well.

"Finally, to all of you," Lord Pendrel continued. "For your loyalty and fealty through many hard years, strange dangers, perhaps some lackluster Lordship—" To which, one and all, we shouted 'no, my lord.' Lord Pendrel held up a hand. "No, we must admit it. There is no harm in it, for we have all fallen short of the glory of Our Father—isn't it written so?" He glanced at me, and I inclined my head. "Whether serf or Lord and Lady, we have each and every one of us suffered from the dragon we ourselves created. But, unless I miss my guess, through the courage of Rae-Anna that dragon is defeated?" There was a twinkle in his eye as he looked at me; so he did remember. I wondered if anyone else did and only hid the knowledge.

I could not say it was because of courage. I certainly felt no courage now, looking back on how I had left Genevieve. And I could not say it was courageous to leave the regret behind and still press forward—was that not the same reasoning I used to leave her in the first place?

And yet, there was still the call for Thomas and I, and one I had tried to abandon at the convent time and time again. I could do so no longer. And so, trusting all to The Beloved, I pressed on. To fail to do so would only add regret on top of regret.

"One may cry in the wilderness 'make straight the way of the Lord,' my lord," I replied. "But it is no small thing to respond to that call in obedience. If there is honor or praise to be given, give it to Him, whose call to mankind never ceases."

"You may indeed ask that, Lady Rae-Anna," he replied. "And yet that obedience may owe itself to the first to obey. And for that, I do confer on you, as within my power, the title of a Lady of Fosse, and Thomas a Lord of Fosse, with all the particulars that grants."

As the hall shouted "Hail, Lord Thomas! Hail, Lady Rae-Anna!" Thomas and I only stared at each other, and tried to formulate some sort of appropriate thanks to Lord and Lady Pendrel. With those titles we could, if necessary and under the authority of the Pendrels themselves, require anyone who had sworn fealty to Fosse to do as we bid—insofar as our commands did not run counter to any standing requirements given by the Pendrels. It meant, in part as well, Thomas and I would be busy in the archives through the rest of winter learning what those standing requirements were. But for the remainder of our stay, if at any time we returned, or even in our travels, anyone sworn to the Pendrels was sworn to us as well.

It was a tremendous honor, and one—given our calling—we would almost never take advantage of. But, in his Lordship's defense, he didn't know that at the time.

Eventually the dinner finished, Lord and Lady Pendrel rising and departing first. It may have been my imagination, but I thought they held hands a little more tenderly as they exited the hall, maybe even walked a little closer together. Certainly they whispered to each other more intimately than I had ever seen them before. The rest of the hall soon emptied in groups. Thomas and I were not far behind, but also had less clear a direction than the others seemed to.

Outside the hall, Mahmoud waited with his hands clasped behind his back. "It will still be a long winter," he observed.

"Yes, I expect so," I replied.

"But there is no more evil?"

I smiled. "There is always evil, Mahmoud, but I understand your question. For our part, I believe we will enjoy castle life for the next few months."

"It will feel almost strange," he said. "You will miss it?"

"The evil?" I asked, sharing a horrified look with Thomas. What did Mahmoud think?

"The fight against it."

"Oh. I don't... I don't look forward to it, I guess..."

"But we don't want to let it keep hurting people," Thomas interjected. "I know I look forward to it only because it means more people set free. At least, I do now. It would be nice to only be a farmer—or maybe a merchant. You get to see more of the world and its people than I would at a farm in Holden." Thomas smiled, and Mahmoud returned it—briefly. "But we have been given the means to fight it, I guess. So hopefully those oppressed by evil can wait another winter."

Mahmoud and I both gazed at him, then at each other. "When he says it like that..." I muttered.

He smiled. "Sorry, that sounded a lot more dire than I meant it.

Obviously we go where and when The Beloved leads us. But unless you have a way over the mountains in the winter?" Mahmoud shook his head. "So, we take our rest for now. I'm sure we'll need it."

"I am sure," Mahmoud replied. "It is a strange thing, but you seem to accept it. Almost easily. It is why I asked."

Thomas and I looked at each other. "Oh no, not easily," I said. "Sometimes it's one of the hardest things—"

"Almost always," Thomas agreed, though he smiled at me. He shrugged. "But it's what is required, and Our Father gives us the strength for it, whatever it is."

"And knowledge," Mahmoud observed.

"Well that was a little newer, and hard to predict," I said. "And certainly we couldn't control it. But, from the beginning we couldn't. He is a living being, after all, with His own will. And He does not always share all knowledge with us."

"Why would He not?"

"I'm not sure. Maybe sometimes answers would only raise more questions. And I think He's very concerned about us relying on ourselves. We try to do it anyway, even without knowing what the next moment will bring. How much more if we felt we had the same knowledge as He does? Could make every decision on our own?"

"Some might say that is a selfish, small god," he said, with a quick nod.

"I didn't think yours was any different," I said with a wry grin. "But no, not selfish. Concerned. If He had not created the earth and sky—if it was just you or I doing it—yes, very selfish. For Him, who knows us and knows what He created, why, and how it works? It seems a supreme act of love to do everything He can to get us to rely on Him."

Mahmoud smiled. "Well enough," he said. He moved off toward

the servants' rooms.

I cocked an eyebrow at Thomas, and we continued on our way as well. "What do you think is next?" I asked as we went on.

"Like you, I think we're done with Castle Fosse—except for your occasional homily," he added with a grin. "So, it will be wherever we move on to next. Maybe Algiers—well, near it. Mahmoud mentioned to me he doesn't go to the city itself, or rarely."

"They won't speak our language there."

"Some will, he said. But no, most will not speak it. That should make it even more interesting."

"Well, as we've said, we just need to keep relying on Him. He'll make a way somehow, for whatever is going on there. What about Mahmoud? Does he seem like he'll continue with us?"

"What, forever?" Thomas chuckled. "No, I think he'll be done outside Algiers. Unless we take up residence there. Do you think we will?"

I hesitated, struggled. "I hope not," I said. "I want to go back to Holden. There are a few people I would like to see again. Maybe even Tabitha, if we can come back through Aurden."

"That would be excellent. All of it. Who all do you want to see?"

"Genevieve."

Thomas put his hand on my arm. "I'm sorry, Rae-Anna. Maybe I shouldn't have told you about her—"

"No, I needed to hear it. I'm sure the convent could have waited. I might have even made it worse for myself by rushing, since Garrett would have attacked the convent at the same time anyway. And so I suffered under Judith for how long before the Fire came to me... And maybe I could have helped Genevieve before I ran off."

"Well. Everything according to Our Father's plan though, right?"

We paused before the door to our chambers. "In this case, I don't think so," I said. "I don't think He has the tight grip on all the events of the world we sometimes think He does. He can obviously redeem it—take our mistakes and work them into His plan just as surely as He works our obedience into it. But does He will that disobedience?" I shook my head. "I can't see that happening. My only hope and prayer now is that He will redeem it, and let me see and maybe even be part of that redemption."

"I can ask Him for that as well," Thomas said. He kissed the top of my head and we went inside.

"I meant to ask you about this Seed you talk about," I said as he shut the door. "I thought you had the Fire the same as I did?"

"Yeah, I've been thinking about that. I wondered if he showed himself as Fire first, so I would know it was the same. But now—I know you talk about the fire, that it shrinks and grows, comforts or warns you, things like that?" I nodded. "Interesting. And it speaks almost directly to you, right?"

"He brings passages of the Holy Words, yes."

"But one at a time?"

"Yes. You mentioned leaves for you—like tree leaves?"

"Yeah. It always sits in there like a seed, sprouting and growing depending on how much he's revealing to me. But I've always enjoyed working through problems like that. So maybe he presents himself that way to me so it's something more familiar. He comes to you through more of a conversation, a relationship. But he comes to me more as a logical puzzle to sort out." He shrugged. "I guess as long as it works itself out the same."

I shook my head. "I don't think I could imagine. I couldn't have made it this far if I had to do it that way."

"And he doesn't make you," he said with a smile. "Isn't that nice of him?"

I laughed. "I guess so."

"It sounds, too, like you have a much more emotional connection to him than I do."

I crinkled my nose. "It does sound that way, doesn't it? Like he's more of a spirit with my spirit, but to you he's more of a plant."

Thomas chuckled. "Well, no plant I know engages my mind the way He does, so don't worry about that." He sobered. "Just make sure... I mean, he promised that he would always be with us. So even if you don't have that little flame you can recognize, that emotional connection, doesn't mean he's not there."

"I know," I said, nodding uncertainly.

"I know you know," he said quickly. "But just...remember I said that, too."

"Thomas, you're worrying me a little bit..."

"Sorry. I just...I felt like it was important to say that."

"O-kay..."

The tightness left his face, as though he'd been lost in thought and just came back. "I'm not sure I like that," he said. "It's not important right this moment. We get to rest for the winter, right?"

I smiled, still a little uncertain though his banter put me at ease. Nothing pressing. "Yes. And more especially tonight, so we can get to the archives first thing in the morning well-rested." I turned away, beginning to undress.

"Rae-Anna?" Thomas asked timidly.

I held back a sigh. I had so hoped... "Yes, Thomas?"

"Is it...is it okay if I watch this time?"

I turned quickly to him. "Ah, yes. Of course!" And suddenly my fingers trembled so much I could barely catch hold of the correct lace.

I hope I have not shared too much of Thomas' and my intimacy, but I felt it was important to show his hurts, and the beginnings of his journey to healing. And my part—and faults—in it, as well. I will not need to write more about it, as from that night on we found, more and more, an ability to live as normal husband and wife—insofar as our work for The Beloved allowed us.

And while Thomas' words of warning would not be important for some time yet, they became a mantra later in my story. But we have an ocean to cross before that tale is ready to be told.

And oceans can be such dangerous places.

Scripture References

Chapter 1:

"Wherefore lift up the hands which hang down, and the feeble knees; ... 15 Looking diligently lest any man fail of the grace of God; lest any root of bitterness springing up trouble [you], and thereby many be defiled;" Heb 12:12, 15

"For he maketh his sun to rise on the evil and on the good, and sendeth rain on the just and on the unjust." Mat 5:45b

Chapter 3:

"The LORD [is] nigh unto them that are of a broken heart; and saveth such as be of a contrite spirit." Psa 34:18

Chapter 4:

"But God hath chosen the foolish things of the world to confound the wise; and God hath chosen the weak things of the world to confound the things which are mighty;" 1Co 1:27

"Drink waters out of thine own cistern, and running waters out of thine own well." Pro 5:15

Chapter 5:

"And the lord said unto the servant, Go out into the highways and hedges, and compel [them] to come in, that my house may be filled. Luk 14:23

"Abstain from all appearance of evil." 1Th 5:22

"That it may be well with thee, and thou mayest live long on the earth." Eph 6:3

"I wrote unto you in an epistle not to company with fornicators: Yet not altogether with the fornicators of this world, or with the covetous, or extortioners, or with idolaters; for then must ye needs go out of the world." 1Co 5:9-10

"How then shall they call on him in whom they have not believed? and how shall they believe in him of whom they have not heard? and how shall they hear without a preacher?" Rom 10:14

Chapter 6:

"And Jesus answered him, 'The first of all the commandments [is], Hear, O Israel; The Lord our God is one Lord:'" Mar 12:29

"'And now, O Father, glorify thou me with thine own self with the glory which I had with thee before the world was.'" Jhn 17:5

"A bruised reed shall he not break, and smoking flax shall he not quench, till he send forth judgment unto victory." Mat 12:20

Chapter 7:

"For I am in a strait betwixt two, having a desire to depart, and to be with Christ; which is far better: Nevertheless to abide in the flesh [is] more needful for you." Phl 1:23-24

"Rejoice with them that do rejoice, and weep with them that weep." Rom 12:15

"And when the servant of the man of God was risen early, and gone forth, behold, an host compassed the city both with horses and chariots. And his servant said unto him, Alas, my master! how shall we do?" 2Ki 6:15

Chapter 8:

"Then said David to the Philistine, 'Thou comest to me with a sword, and with a spear, and with a shield: but I come to thee in the name of the LORD of hosts, the God of the armies of Israel, whom thou hast defied.'" 1Sa 17:45

"Purge me with hyssop, and I shall be clean: wash me, and I shall be whiter than snow." Psa 51:7

Chapter 11:

"'Take therefore no thought for the morrow: for the morrow shall take thought for the things of itself. Sufficient unto the day [is] the evil thereof.'" Mat 6:34

"But many of the priests and Levites and chief of the fathers, [who were] ancient men, that had seen the first house, when the foundation of this house was laid before their eyes, wept with a loud voice; and many shouted aloud for joy:" Ezr 3:12

Chapter 12:

"If I ascend up into heaven, thou [art] there: if I make my bed in hell, behold, thou [art there]." Psa 139:8

"Judge not, and ye shall not be judged: condemn not, and ye shall not be condemned: forgive, and ye shall be forgiven: ... For a good tree bringeth not forth corrupt fruit; neither doth a corrupt tree bring forth good fruit." Luk 6:37, 43

"Make me to hear joy and gladness; [that] the bones [which] thou hast broken may rejoice." Psa 51:8

Chapter 13:

"And they that are Christ's have crucified the flesh with the affections and lusts." Gal 5:24

Chapter 14:

"'For the Holy Ghost shall teach you in the same hour what ye ought to say.'" Luk 12:12

"The people which sat in darkness saw great light; and to them which sat in the region and shadow of death light is sprung up." Mat 4:16

"The Lord is not slack concerning his promise, as some men count slackness; but is longsuffering to us-ward, not willing that any should perish, but that all should come to repentance." 2Pe 3:9

"But to Israel he saith, 'All day long I have stretched forth my hands unto a disobedient and gainsaying people.' ... How then shall they call on him in whom they have not believed? and how shall they believe in him of whom they have not heard? and how shall they hear without a preacher?" Rom 10:21, 14

Prayer Times

Pre-Dawn—Nebuls

Dawn—Gemmans

Morning—Quard

Noon Meal—Lentus

Afternoon—Aratus

Dinner—Scuros

Nightfall—Lunens

Midnight—Somnus

About the Author

Daniel Dydek is a multi-genre author with his sweeping epic fantasy series The Triumvirs, and his supernatural suspense series, Spirit Wind, has already garnered two Finalist awards from Realm Makers. Besides writing, he also enjoys a personal relationship with Jesus Christ, mountain biking, reading, coffee shops, book stores, and Durango Colorado. He lives in Canton Ohio with his wife and son and two cats.

Support for the Author

First, thank you for reading this story on whichever medium you chose—Kindle, KU, or paperback. Your support means dreams come true! If you loved the story, there are a lot of ways to continue supporting the author FOR FREE. Here's a few:

1. Subscribe to the newsletter on danieldydek.com

2. Tell your friends!

3. Leave a review on Goodreads, Amazon, Barnes & Noble, or on your social media. (This is probably the greatest support of all, because we love hearing what people enjoyed about the book! Plus, you know, algorithms...)

4. Request your local library to get a copy

All these things help promote the books, and encourage the author to keep writing stories you'll love!

—The Beorn Publishing Team

The Triumvirs epic fantasy series

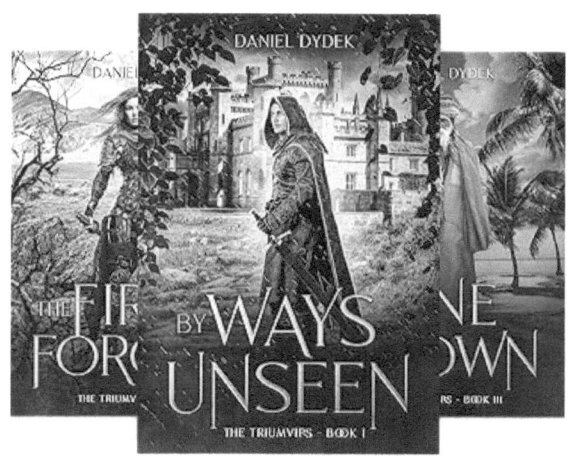

Centuries ago, the world of Oren was ravaged by uncontrolled magic during the Wizards War. In the wake of such devastation and evil, the God of All took three wizards and established for them a Room, of darkness and consciousness, and placed before them a great table whose appearance is of translucent slate, through which they might call up visions of the lands, entering when needed. Few even know these former wizards exist, and their work will always be credited to brave men and women of the world who were faithful in their obedience.

These wizards' task is keeping the peace, of prompting action against the forces of evil. They answer still to the God of All, but retain autonomy. He named them The Triumvirate, and over the centuries twenty-two Triumvirs have guided Oren through wars, famines, pestilences, and the rising and falling of countless empires.

Now, in this current Age of men, will come their most difficult battle.

Amazon search: The Triumvirs Dydek

Spirit Wind **Christian suspense series**

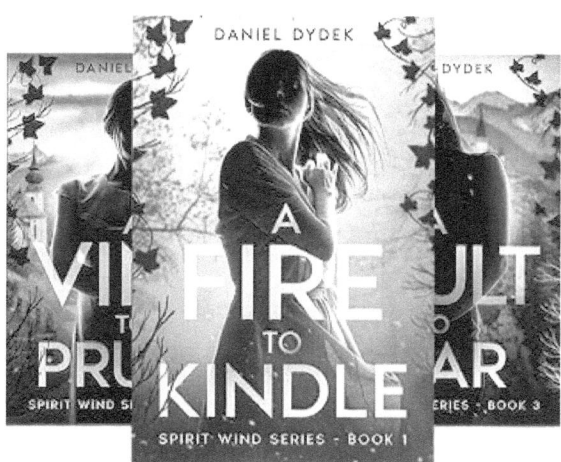

Cursed with left-handedness, then cursed with fire.

Except the fire seems to comfort, to strengthen, to speak wisdom. Wisdom like:

"The wind bloweth where it listeth, and thou hearest the sound thereof, but canst not tell whence it cometh, and whither it goeth: so is every one that is born of the Spirit."

And so Rae-Anna is borne on itinerant winds, never knowing what danger she'll be asked to face. But she knows this: it will always be demonic. And she will never be alone.

Amazon search: Spirit Wind Dydek